Pushkin Hills

Pushkin Hills

Sergei Dovlatov

Translated by Katherine Dovlatov

Afterword by James Wood

COUNTERPOINT
BERKELEY

Library of Congress Cataloging-in-Publication Data
Dovlatov, Sergei.
Pushkin hills / Sergei Dovlatov; translated by Katherine Dovlatov
[with afterword, by] James Wood.
    pages cm.
Translated from Russian to English.
ISBN 978-1-61902-245-4 (hardback)
I. Wood, James. II. Title.
PG3479.6.O85P8713 2014
891.73'44—DC23
                    2013028859

Cover design by Natalya Balnova
Author photo © Nina Alovert, 1980

COUNTERPOINT
1919 Fifth Street
Berkeley, CA 94710
www.counterpointpress.com

Printed in the United States of America
Distributed by Publishers Group West

10 9 8 7 6 5 4 3 2 1

Contents

Pushkin Hills

To my wife, who was right

A T NOON WE PULLED INTO LUGA. We stopped at the
station square and the tour guide adjusted her tone from
a lofty to an earthier one:

"There to the left are the facilities…"

My neighbour pricked up his ears:

"You mean the restroom?"

He had been nagging me the entire trip: "A bleaching agent,
six letters? An endangered artiodactyl? An Austrian downhill
skier?"

The tourists exited onto a sunlit square. The driver slammed
the door shut and crouched by the radiator.

The station: a dingy yellow building with columns, a clock
tower and flickering neon letters, faded by the sun…

I cut across the vestibule with its newspaper stand and mas-
sive cement urns and instinctively sought out a café.

"Through the waiter," grumbled the woman at the counter.
A bottle-opener dangled on her fallen bosom.

I sat by the door. A waiter with tremendous felted sideburns
materialized a minute later.

"What's your pleasure?"

"My pleasure," I said, "is for everyone to be kind, humble
and courteous."

The waiter, having had his fill of life's diversity, said nothing.

"My pleasure is half a glass of vodka, a beer and two
sandwiches."

"What kind?"

"Sausage, I guess."

I got out a pack of cigarettes and lit up. My hands were shaking uncontrollably. "Better not drop the glass..." And just then two refined old ladies sat down at the next table. They looked like they were from our bus.

The waiter brought a small carafe, a bottle of beer and two chocolates.

"The sandwiches are all gone," he announced with a note of false tragedy.

I paid up. I lifted the glass and put it down right away. My hands shook like an epileptic's. The old ladies looked me over with distaste. I attempted a smile:

"Look at me with love!"

The ladies shuddered and changed tables. I heard some muffled interjections of disapproval.

To hell with them, I thought. I steadied the glass with both hands and drained it. Then I wrestled out the sweet.

I began to feel better. That deceptive feeling of bliss was setting in. I stuffed the beer in my pocket and stood up, nearly knocking over the chair. A Duralumin armchair, to be precise. The old ladies continued to scrutinize me with apprehension.

I stepped onto the square. Its walls were covered with warped plywood billboards. The drawings promised mountains of meat, wool, eggs and various unmentionables in the not-too-distant future.

The men were smoking by the side of the bus. The women were noisily taking their seats. The tour guide was eating an ice cream in the shade. I approached her:

"Let's get acquainted."

"Aurora," she said, extending a sticky hand.

"And I am," I said, "Borealis."

The girl didn't take offence.

"Everyone makes fun of my name. I'm used to it... What's wrong with you? You're all red!"

"I assure you, it's only on the outside. On the inside I'm a constitutional democrat."

"No, really, are you unwell?"

"I drink too much... Would you like a beer?"

"Why do you drink?" she asked.

What could I say?

"It's a secret," I said, "a little mystery..."

"So you've decided to work at the museum?"

"Exactly."

"I knew it right away."

"Do I look like the literary type?"

"Mitrofanov was seeing you off. He's an extremely learned Pushkin scholar. Are you good friends?"

"I'm good friends," I said, "with his bad side..."

"How do you mean?"

"Never mind."

"You should read Gordin, Shchegolev, Tsyavlovskaya... Kern's memoirs...* and one of the popular brochures on the dangers of alcohol."

"You know, I've read so much about the dangers of alcohol that I decided to give it up... reading, that is."

"You're impossible to talk to."

7

The driver glanced in our direction. The tourists were in their seats.

Aurora finished the ice cream and wiped her fingers.

"In the summer," she said, "the museum pays very well. Mitrofanov makes close to two hundred roubles."

"And that's two hundred roubles more than he's worth."

"Why, you're also bitter."

"You'd be bitter too," I said.

The driver honked twice.

"Let's go," said Aurora.

The Lvov bus was stuffy. The calico seats were burning hot. The yellow curtains intensified the feeling of suffocation.

I was leafing through the pages of Alexei Vulf's *Diaries*.* They referred to Pushkin in a friendly and sometimes condescending manner. There it was, the closeness that spoils vision. Everyone knows that geniuses must have friends. But who'll believe that his friend is a genius?!

I dozed off to the murmur of some unintelligible and irrelevant facts about Ryleyev's mother...*

Someone woke me when we were already in Pskov. The kremlin's freshly plastered walls brought on a feeling of gloom. The designers had secured a grotesque Baltic-style emblem made of wrought iron above the central archway. The kremlin resembled a gigantic model.

One of the outbuildings housed the local travel bureau. Aurora filed some paperwork and we were driven to Hera, the most fashionable local restaurant.

I wavered – to top up or not? If I drank more, tomorrow it'd be even worse. I didn't feel like eating...

I walked onto the boulevard. Low and heavy, the lindens rustled.

Long ago I realized that as soon as you give way to thinking, you remember something sad. For instance, my last conversation with my wife...

"Even your love of words – your crazy, unhealthy, pathological love – is fake. It's nothing more than an attempt to justify the life you lead. And you lead the life of a famous writer without fulfilling the slightest requirements. With your vices you should be a Hemingway at the very least..."

"Do you honestly think he's a good writer? Perhaps Jack London's a good writer, too?"

"Dear God! What does Jack London have to do with this?! My only pair of boots is in the pawnshop... I can forgive anything. Poverty doesn't scare me. Anything but betrayal!"

"What do you mean?"

"Your endless drinking. Your... I don't even want to say it... You can't be an artist at the expense of another human being... It's low! You speak of nobility, yet you are a cold, hard and crafty man..."

"Don't forget that I've been writing stories for twenty years."

"You want to write a great novel? Only one in a hundred million succeeds!"

"So what? In the spiritual sense a failed attempt like that is equal to the greatest of books. Morally it's even higher, if you will, since it excludes a reward..."

"These are just words. Never-ending, beautiful words... I've had enough... I have a child for whom I'm responsible..."

"I have a child, too."

"Whom you ignore for months on end. We are strangers to you..."

(In conversations with women there is one painful moment. You use facts, reasoning, arguments, you appeal to logic and common sense. And then suddenly you discover that she cannot stand the very sound of your voice...)

"Intentionally," I said, "I never did any harm..."

I sat down on a sloping bench, pulled out a pen and a piece of paper, and a minute later scribbled down:

My darling, I'm in Pushkin Hills now,
Monotony and boredom without a switch,
I wander through the grounds like a bitch,
And fear is wracking my very soul!

And so on.

My verses had somewhat preceded reality. We still had about a hundred kilometres to Pushkin Hills.

I stopped by a convenience store and bought an envelope that had Magellan's portrait on it. And asked, for some reason:

"Do you know what Magellan has to do with anything?"

The sales clerk replied pensively:

"Maybe he died... Or got decorated..."

I licked the stamp, sealed the envelope and dropped it in the mailbox...

At six we reached the tourist centre. Before that there were hills, a river, the sweeping horizon with a jagged trim of forest. All in all, a typical Russian landscape without excess. Just those ordinary features that evoke an inexplicably bittersweet feeling.

This feeling had always seemed suspect to me. In general, I find passion towards inanimate objects irritating. (Mentally I opened a notepad.) There is something amiss in coin collectors, philatelists, inveterate travellers and lovers of cactuses and aquarium fish. The sleepy forbearance of a fisherman, the futile, unmotivated bravery of a mountain climber and the haughty confidence of the owner of a royal poodle are all alien to me.

They say that the Jews are indifferent to nature. That's one of the grievances levelled against the Jewish nation. The Jews, supposedly, don't have their own nature, and they're indifferent to everyone else's. Perhaps that's true. It would seem that the bit of Jewish blood in me is beginning to show.

In short, I don't like exalted spectators. And I am mistrustful of their rapture. I believe that their love of birch trees triumphs at the expense of the love of mankind. And grows as a surrogate for patriotism.

I agree, you feel love and pity for your mother more acutely if she is sick or paralysed. However, to admire her suffering, to express it aesthetically, is low.

But enough...

We drove up to the tourist centre. Some idiot built it four kilometres away from the nearest water supply. Ponds, lakes, a famous river – but the centre is right under the blazing sun. Though there are rooms with showers and occasionally hot water...

We walked into the main office. There was a woman sitting there, a retired soldier's dream. Aurora handed her the register, signed some papers and picked up food vouchers for the group. Then she whispered something to this curvy blonde who immediately shot me a glance. The look expressed a harsh, cursory interest, businesslike concern and mild alarm. She even sat up straighter. Her papers rustled with more of a snap.

"Have you met?" asked Aurora.

I stepped forward.

"I'd like to work at the Pushkin Preserve."

"We need people…" replied the blonde.

The ellipsis at the end of this rejoinder was palpable. In other words, only good, qualified specialists are needed; random people need not apply…

"Are you familiar with the collection?" asked the blonde, and suddenly introduced herself. "Galina Alexandrovna."

"I've been here two or three times."

"That's not enough."

"I agree. So here I am again…"

"You need to prepare properly. Thoroughly study the guidebooks. So much in Pushkin's life is waiting to be discovered. Certain things have changed since last year…"

"In Pushkin's life?" I marvelled.

"Excuse me," interrupted Aurora. "The tourists are waiting. Good luck."

And she disappeared – young, wholesome, full of life. Tomorrow I will hear her pure girlish voice in one of the museum's rooms:

"...Just think, comrades!... 'I love you so truly, so tenderly...' – Pushkin contrasted this inspired hymn to selflessness with the mores of the serf-owning world..."

"Not in Pushkin's life," the blonde said irritably, "but in the layout of the collection. For instance, they took down the portrait of Hannibal."

"Why?"

"Some busybody insisted it wasn't Hannibal. The medals, you see, don't match. Supposedly, it's General Zakomelsky."*

"So who is it really?"

"Really it's Zakomelsky."

"Then why is he black?"

"He fought with the Asians in the south. It's hot there, so he got a tan. Plus the paints get darker with age."

"So they were right to take it down?"

"Oh, what's the difference – Hannibal or Zakomelsky?... The tourists came to see Hannibal. They paid money. What in hell do they need Zakomelsky for?! And so our director hung up Hannibal. I mean Zakomelsky masquerading as Hannibal. And some character didn't like it. Excuse me, are you married?"

Galina Alexandrovna uttered this phrase suddenly – and shyly, I'd add.

"Divorced," I said. "Why?"

"Our girls are interested."

"What girls?"

"They're not here now. The accountant, the methodologist, the tour guides..."

"And why are they interested in me?"

"They're not interested in you. They're interested in everyone. There are a lot of single girls here. The guys left... Who do our girls get to see? The tourists? And what about the tourists? It's good if they stay a week. The ones from Leningrad stop overnight. Or just for the weekend. How long will you be here?"

"Till autumn. If all goes well."

"Where are you staying? Would you like me to call the hotel? We have two of them, a good one and a bad one. Which do you prefer?"

"That," I told her, "requires some thought."

"The good one's expensive," explained Galina.

"All right," I said, "I've no money anyway."

She immediately dialled somewhere and pleaded with someone for a long time. Finally the matter was settled. Somewhere someone wrote down my name.

"I'll take you there."

It had been a while since I'd been the object of such intense female concern. It would prove to be even more insistent in the future, escalating into pressure.

At first I attributed it to my tarnished individuality. Later I discovered just how acute the shortage of males in these parts was. A bow-legged local tractor driver with the tresses of a train-station floozie was always surrounded by pushy pink-cheeked admirers.

"I'm dying for a beer!" he'd whine.

And the girls ran for beer...

Galina locked the door of the main office. We proceeded through the woods towards the settlement.

"Do you love Pushkin?" she asked me unexpectedly. Something in me winced, but I replied:

"I love... *The Bronze Horseman,** his prose..."

"And what about the poems?"

"His later poems I love very much."

"And what about the earlier ones?"

"The earlier ones too," I surrendered.

"Everything here lives and breathes Pushkin," continued Galina. "Literally every twig, every blade of grass. You can't help but expect him to come out from around the corner... The top hat, the cloak, that familiar profile..."

Meanwhile, it was Lenya Guryanov, a former college snitch, who appeared from around the corner.

"Boris, you giant dildo," he bellowed, "is it really you?!"

I replied with surprising amiability. Yet another lowlife had caught me unawares. I'm always too slow to gather my thoughts...

"I knew you'd come," Guryanov went on.

Later I was told this story. There was a big booze-up at the beginning of the season. Someone's wedding or birthday. One of the guests was a local KGB officer. My name came up in conversation. One of our mutual friends said:

"He's in Tallinn."

Someone countered:

"No, he's been in Leningrad at least a year."

"I heard he was in Riga, staying at Krasilnikov's..."

More and more versions followed. The KGB agent stayed

focused on the braised duck. Then he lifted his head and stated brusquely:

"There's intel that he's getting ready for Pushkin Hills..."

"I'm late," said Guryanov, as if I was keeping him.

He turned to Galina:

"You're looking good. Don't tell me, did you get new teeth?"

His pockets bulged heavily.

"You little prick!" blurted Galina. And the next minute:

"It's a good thing Pushkin isn't here to see this."

"Yes," I said, "it's not a bad thing."

The first floor of the Friendship Hotel was home to three establishments: a general store, a hairdresser's and the restaurant The Seashore. I should, I thought, invite Galina to dinner for all her help. But my funds were appallingly low. One grand gesture could end in catastrophe.

I kept quiet.

We walked up to the barrier, behind which sat the administrator. Galina introduced me. The woman extended a chunky key with the number 231.

"And tomorrow you can find a room," said Galina. "Perhaps in the settlement... Or in Voronich, but it's expensive... Or you can look in one of the nearby villages: Savkino, Gaiki..."

"Thank you," I said. "You've been a great help."

"So, I'll be going then."

The words ended with a barely audible question mark: "So, I'll be going then?"

"Shall I walk you home?"

"I live in the housing development," the young woman responded mysteriously.

And then – distinctly and clearly, very distinctly and very clearly:

"There's no need to walk me... And don't get any ideas, I'm not that type..."

She gave the administrator a proud nod and strutted away.

I climbed to the second floor and opened the door. The bed was neatly made. The loudspeaker sputtered intermittently. The hangers swung on the crossbar of an open built-in closet.

In this room, in this narrow dinghy, I was setting sail for the distant shores of my independent bachelor life.

I showered, washing away the ticklish residue of Galina's attentions, the sticky coating of a crammed bus, the lamina of many days of drinking.

My mood improved noticeably. A cold shower worked like a loud scream.

I dried myself, put on a pair of tracksuit bottoms and lit a cigarette.

Footsteps shuffled down the hall. Somewhere music was playing. Trucks and countless mopeds caused a ruckus outside the window.

I lay on top of the duvet and opened a little grey volume by Victor Likhonosov.* I decided it was time to find out exactly what this village prose was, to arm myself with a sort of guide...

While reading, I fell asleep. When I woke up it was two in the morning. The shadowy light of summer dawn filled the room. You could already count the leaves of the rubber plant on the window sill.

I decided to think things through calmly, to try and get rid of the feeling of catastrophe and deadlock.

Life spread out before me as an immeasurable minefield and I was at its centre. It was time to divide this field into lots and get down to business. To break the chain of dramatic events, to analyse the feeling of failure, to examine each aspect in isolation.

A man has been writing stories for twenty years. He is convinced that he picked up the pen for a reason. People he trusts are ready to attest to this.

You are not being published. You are not welcomed into their circles, into their band of bandits. But is that really what you dreamt of when you mumbled your first lines?

You want justice? Relax, that fruit doesn't grow here. A few shining truths were supposed to change the world for the better, but what really happened?

You have a dozen readers and you should pray to God for fewer...

You don't make any money – now that's not good. Money is freedom, space, caprice... Money makes poverty bearable...

You must learn to make money without being a hypocrite. Go work as a stevedore and do your writing at night. Mandelstam* said that people will preserve what they need. So write...

You have some ability – you might not have. Write. Create a masterpiece. Give your reader a revelation. One single living person... That's the goal of a lifetime.

And what if you don't succeed? Well, you've said it yourself – morally, a failed attempt is even more noble, if only because it is unrewarded...

Write, since you picked up the pen, and bear this burden. The heavier it is, the easier...

You are weighed down by debts? Name someone who hasn't been! Don't let it upset you. After all, it's the only bond that really connects you to other people.

Looking around, do you see ruins? That was to be expected. He who lives in the world of words does not get along with things.

You envy anyone who calls himself a writer, anyone who can present a legal document with proof of that fact.

But let's look at what your contemporaries have written. You've stumbled on the following in the writer Volin's work;*

"It became comprehensibly clear to me..."

And on the same page:

"With incomprehensible clarity Kim felt..."

A word is turned upside down. Its contents fall out. Or rather, it turns out it didn't have any. Words piled intangibly, like the shadow of an empty bottle...

But that's not the point! I'm so tired of your constant manipulation!

Life is impossible. You must either live or write. Either the word or business. But the word is your business. And you detest all Business with a capital B. It is surrounded by empty, dead space. It destroys everything that interferes with your business. It destroys hopes, dreams and memories. It is ruled by contemptible, incontrovertible and unequivocal materialism.

And again – that's not the point!

What have you done to your wife? She was trusting, flirtatious and fun-loving. You made her jealous, suspicious and neurotic. Her persistent response: "What do you mean by that?" is a monument to your cunning...

Your outrageousness borders on the extraordinary. Do you remember when you came home around four o'clock in the morning and began undoing your shoelaces? Your wife woke up and groaned:

"Dear God, where are you off to at this hour?!"

"You're right, you're right, it's too early," you mumbled, undressed quickly and lay down.

Oh, what more is there to say?

Morning. Footsteps muffled by the crimson runner. Abrupt sputtering of the loudspeaker. The splash of water next door. Trucks outside. The startling call of a rooster somewhere in the distance.

In my childhood the sound of summer was marked by the whistling of steam engines... Country dachas... The smell of burnt coal and hot sand... Table tennis under the trees... The taut and clear snap of the ball... Dancing on the veranda (your older cousin trusted you to wind the gramophone)... Gleb Romanov... Ruzhena Sikora... "This song for two *soldi*, this song for two pennies...", 'I Daydreamt of You in Bucharest...'*

The beach burnt by the sun... The rugged sedge... Long bathing trunks and elastic marks on your calves... Sand in your shoes...

Someone knocked on the door:

"Telephone!"

"That must be a mistake," I said.

"Are you Alikhanov?"

I was shown to the housekeeper's room. I picked up the receiver.

"Were you sleeping?" asked Galina.

I protested emphatically.

I noticed that people respond to this question with excessive fervour. Ask a person, "Do you go on benders?" and he will calmly say, "No." Or, perhaps, agree readily. But ask, "Were you sleeping?" and the majority will be upset as if insulted. As if they were implicated in a crime.

"I've made arrangements for a room."

"Well, thank you."

"It's in a village called Sosnovo. Five minutes away from the tourist centre. And it has a private entrance."

"That's key."

"Although the landlord drinks..."

"Yet another bonus."

"Remember his name – Sorokin. Mikhail Ivanych... Walk through the tourist centre, along the ravine. You'll be able to see the village from the hill. Fourth house. Or maybe the fifth. I'm sure you'll find it. There's a dump next to it."

"Thank you, darling."

Her tone changed abruptly.

"Darling?! You're killing me... Darling... Honestly... So, he's found himself a darling..."

Later on, I'd often be astonished by Galina's sudden transformations. Lively involvement, kindness and sincerity gave way to shrill inflections of offended virtue. Her normal voice was replaced by a piercing provincial dialect...

"And don't get any ideas!"

"Ideas – never. And once again – thank you..."

I headed to the tourist centre. This time it was full of people. Colourful automobiles were parked all around. Tourists in sun hats ambled in groups and on their own. A line had formed by the newspaper kiosk. The clatter of crockery and the screeching of metallic stools came through the wide-open windows of the cafeteria. A few well-fed mutts romped around in the middle of it all.

A picture of Pushkin greeted me everywhere I looked. Even near the mysterious little brick booth with the "Inflammable!" sign. The similarity was confined to the sideburns. Their amplitude varied indiscriminately. I noticed long ago that our artists favour certain objects that place no restriction on the scale or the imagination. At the top of the list are Karl Marx's beard and Lenin's forehead...

The loudspeaker was on at full volume:

"Attention! You are listening to the Pushkin Hills tourist-centre broadcasting station. Here is today's schedule of activities..."

I walked into the main office. Galina was beset by tourists. She motioned me to wait.

I picked up the brochure *Pearl of the Crimea* from the shelf and took out my cigarettes.

After collecting some paperwork, the tour guides would leave. The tourists ran after them to the buses. Several "stray" families wanted to join a group. They were being looked after by a tall, slender girl.

A man in a Tyrolean hat approached me timidly.

"My apologies, may I ask you a question?"

"Go ahead."

"Is that the expanse?"

"What do you mean?"

"I am asking you, is that the expanse?" The Tyrolean dragged me to an open window.

"In what sense?"

"In the most obvious. I would like to know whether that is the expanse or not? If it isn't the expanse, just say so."

"I don't understand."

The man turned slightly red and began to explain, hurriedly:

"I had a postcard... I am a cartophilist..."

"Who?"

"A cartophilist. I collect postcards... *Philos* – love, *cartos*..."

"OK, got it."

"I own a colour postcard titled *The Pskov Expanse*. And now that I'm here I want to know – is that the expanse?"

"I don't see why not," I said.

"Typical Pskovian?"

"You bet."

The man walked away, beaming.

The rush hour was over and the centre emptied.

"Each summer there's a larger influx of tourists," explained Galina.

And then, raising her voice slightly: "The prophecy came true: 'The sacred path will not be overgrown...'!"*

No, I think not. How could it get overgrown, the poor thing, being trampled by squadrons of tourists?...

"Mornings here are a total clusterfuck," said Galina.

And once again I was surprised by the unexpected turn of her language.

Galina introduced me to the office instructor, Lyudmila. I would secretly admire her smooth legs till the end of the season. Luda had an even and friendly temperament. This was explained by the existence of a fiancé. She hadn't been marred by a constant readiness to make an angry rebuff. For now her fiancé was in jail...

Shortly after, an unattractive woman of about thirty appeared: the methodologist. Her name was Marianna Petrovna. Marianna had a neglected face without defects and an imperceptibly bad figure.

I explained my reason for being there. With a sceptical smile, she invited me to follow her to the office.

"Do you love Pushkin?"

I felt a muffled irritation.

"I do."

At this rate, I thought, it won't be long before I don't.

"And may I ask you why?"

I caught her ironic glance. Evidently the love of Pushkin was the most widely circulated currency in these parts. What if I were a counterfeiter, God forbid?

"What do you mean?" I asked.

"Why do you love Pushkin?"

"Let's stop this idiotic test," I burst out. "I graduated from school. And from university." (Here I exaggerated a bit; I was expelled in my third year.) "I've read a few books. In short, I have a basic understanding… Besides, I'm only seeking a job as a tour guide…"

Luckily, my snap response went unnoticed. As I later learnt, basic rudeness was easier to get away with here than feigned aplomb.

"And nevertheless?" Marianna waited for an answer. What's more, she waited for a specific answer she had been expecting.

"OK," I said, "I'll give it a try… Here we go… Pushkin is our belated Renaissance. Like Goethe was for Weimar. They took upon themselves what the West had mastered in the fifteenth, sixteenth and seventeenth centuries. Pushkin found a way to express social themes in the form of tragedy, a characteristic of the Renaissance. He and Goethe lived, if you will, in several eras. *Werther* is a tribute to sentimentalism. *Prisoner of the Caucasus* is a typically Byronesque work. But *Faust*, for instance – that's already Elizabethan and the *Little Tragedies* naturally continue one of the Renaissance genres. The same with Pushkin's lyricism. And if it's dark, then it isn't dark in the spirit of Byron but more in the spirit of Shakespeare's sonnets, I feel. Am I explaining myself clearly?"

"What has Goethe got to do with anything?" asked Marianna. "And the same goes for the Renaissance!"

"Nothing!" I finally exploded. "Goethe has absolutely nothing to do with this! And 'Renaissance' was the name of Don Quixote's horse. And it too has nothing to do with this! And evidently I have nothing to do with this either!"

"Please calm down," whispered Marianna. "You're a bundle

of nerves… I only asked, 'Why do you love Pushkin?'"

"To love publicly is obscene!" I yelled. "There is a special term for it in sexual pathology!"

With a shaking hand she extended me a glass of water. I pushed it away.

"Have you loved anyone? Ever?!"

I shouldn't have said it. Now she'll break down and start screaming: "I am thirty-four years old and I am single!"

"Pushkin is our pride and joy!" managed Marianna. "He is not only a great poet, he is also Russia's great citizen…"

Apparently this was the prepared answer to her idiotic question.

And that's it? I thought.

"Do look at the guidelines. Also, here is a list of books. They are available in the reading room. And report to Galina Alexandrovna that the interview went well."

I felt embarrassed.

"Thank you," I said. "I'm sorry I lost my temper."

I rolled up the brochure and put it in my pocket.

"Be careful with it – we only have three copies."

I took the papers out and attempted to smooth them with my hands.

"And one more thing," Marianna lowered her voice. "You asked about love…"

"It was you who asked about love."

"No, it was you who asked about love… As I understand, you are interested in whether I am married? Well, I am!"

"You have robbed me of my last hope," I said as I was leaving.

In the hallway Galina introduced me to Natella, another guide. And another unexpected burst of interest:

"You'll be working here?"

"I'll try."

"Do you have cigarettes?"

We stepped onto the porch.

Natella had come from Moscow at the urge of romantic, or rather reckless ideas. A physicist by education, she worked as a schoolteacher. She decided to spend her three-month holiday here. And regretted coming. The Preserve was total pandemonium. The tour guides and methodologists were nuts. The tourists were ignorant pigs. And everyone was crazy about Pushkin. Crazy about their love for Pushkin. Crazy about their love for their love. The only decent person was Markov...

"Who is Markov?"

"A photographer. And a hopeless drunk. I'll introduce you. He taught me to drink Agdam.* It's out of this world. He can teach you too...,"

"Much obliged. But I'm afraid that in that department I myself am an expert."

"Then let's knock some back one day! Right here in the lap of nature..."

"Agreed."

"I see you are a dangerous man."

"How do you mean?"

"I sensed it right away. You are a terribly dangerous man."

"When I'm not sober?"

"That's not what I'm talking about."

"I don't understand."

"To fall in love with someone like you is dangerous."

And Natella gave me an almost painful nudge with her knee. Christ, I thought, everyone here is insane. Even those who find everyone else insane.

"Have some Agdam," I said, "and calm down. I want to get some rest and do a little work. I pose you no danger..."

"We'll see about that." And Natella broke into hysterical laughter.

She coquettishly swung her canvas bag with an image of James Bond on it and walked off.

I set off for Sosnovo. The road stretched to the top of the hill, skirting a cheerless field. Dark boulders loomed along its edges in shapeless piles. A ravine, thick with brush, gaped on the left. Coming downhill, I saw several log houses girdled by birch trees. Monochrome cows milled about on the side, flat like theatre decorations. Grimy sheep with decadent expressions grazed lazily on the grass. Jackdaws circled above the roofs.

I walked through the village hoping to come across someone. Unpainted grey houses looked squalid. Clay pots crowned the pickets of sagging fences. Baby chicks clamoured in the plastic-covered coops. Chickens pranced around in a nervous, strobing strut. Squat, shaggy dogs yipped gamely.

I crossed the village and walked back, pausing near one of the houses. A door slammed and a man in a faded railroad tunic appeared on the front steps.

I asked where I could find Sorokin.

"They call me Tolik," he said.

I introduced myself and once again explained that I was looking for Sorokin.

"Where does he live?"

"In the village of Sosnovo."

"But this is Sosnovo."

"I know. How can I find him?"

"D'ya mean Timokha Sorokin?"

"His name is Mikhail Ivanych."

"Timokha's been dead a year. He froze, havin' partaken..."

"I'd really like to find Sorokin."

"Didn't partake enough, I say, or he'da still been here."

"What about Sorokin?"

"You don't mean Mishka, by chance?"

"His name is Mikhail Ivanych."

"Well, that'd be Mishka all right. Dolikha's son-in-law. D'ya know Dolikha, the one that's a brick short of a load?"

"I'm not from around here."

"Not from Opochka, by chance?"

"From Leningrad."

"Ah, yeah, I heard of it..."

"So how do I find Mikhail Ivanych?"

"You mean Mishka?"

"Precisely."

Tolik relieved himself from the steps deliberately and without reservation. Then he cracked open the door and piped a command:

"Ahoy! Bonehead Ivanych! You got a visitor!"

He winked and added:

"It's the cops for the alimony..."

A crimson muzzle, generously adorned with blue eyes, appeared momentarily.

"Whatsa... Who?... You about the gun?"

"I was told you have a room to let."

The expression on Mikhail Ivanych's face betrayed deep confusion. I would later discover that this was his normal reaction to any question, however harmless.

"A room?... Whatsa... Why?"

"I work at the Preserve. I'd like to rent a room. Temporarily. Till autumn. Do you have a spare room?"

"The house is Ma's. In her name. And Ma's in Pskov. Her feet swolled up."

"So you don't have a room?"

"Jews had it last year. I got no complaints, the people had class... No furniture polish, no cologne... Just red, white and beer... Me personally, I respect the Jews."

"They put Christ on the cross," interjected Tolik.

"That was ages ago!" yelled Mikhail Ivanych. "Long before the Revolution."

"The room," I said. "Is it for rent or not?"

"Show the man," commanded Tolik, zipping his fly.

The three of us walked down a village street. A woman was standing by a fence, wearing a man's jacket with the Order of the Red Star* pinned to the lapel.

"Zin, lend me a fiver," belted out Mikhail Ivanych.

The woman waved him away.

"Wine'll be the death of you... Have ya heard, they got a new decree out? To string up every wino with cable!"

"Where?!" Mikhail Ivanych guffawed. "They'll run outta metal. Our entire metalworks will go bust..."

And he added:

"You old tart. Just wait, you'll come to me for wood... I work at the forestry. I'm a *Friendshipist*!"

"What?" I didn't understand.

"I got a power saw... one from the 'Friendship' line... Whack – and there's a tenner in my pocket."

"Friendshipist," grumbled the woman. "Your only friend's the big swill... See you don't drink yourself into the box..."

"It's not that easy," said Mikhail Ivanych almost regretfully.

This was a broad-shouldered, well-built man. Even tatty, filthy clothes could not truly disfigure him. A weathered face, large, protruding collarbones under an open shirt, a steady, confident stride... I couldn't help but admire him...

Mikhail Ivanych's house made a horrifying impression. A sloping antenna shone black against the white clouds. Sections of the roof had caved in, revealing dark, uneven beams. The walls were carelessly covered in plywood. The cracked window panes were held together with newspaper. Filthy oakum poked out from the countless gaps.

The stench of rotten food hung in the owner's room. Over the table I noticed a coloured portrait of General Mao, torn from a magazine. Next to him beamed Gagarin.* Pieces of noodles were swimming in the sink with dark circles of chipped enamel. The wall clock was silent: an old pressing iron, used as weight on the main wheel, rested on the floor.

Two heraldic-looking cats – one charcoal-black, the other pinkish-white – sauntered haughtily about the table, weaving past the plates. The owner shooed them away with a felt boot that came to hand. Glass smashed. The cats fled into a dark corner with a piercing howl.

The room next door was even more disgusting. The middle of the ceiling sagged dangerously low. Two metal beds were hidden under tattered clothes and putrid sheepskins. The surfaces were covered with cigarette butts and eggshells.

To be honest, I was at a bit of a loss. If only I could have simply said: "I'm afraid this won't work…" But it appears I am genteel after all. And so I said something lyrical:

"The windows face south?"

"The very, very south," Tolik affirmed.

Through the window I saw a dilapidated bathhouse.

"The main thing," I said, "is that there's a private entrance."

"The entrance is private," agreed Mikhail Ivanych, "only it's nailed shut."

"Oh, that's too bad," I said.

"*Ein Moment*," said the owner, took a few steps back, and charged the door.

"What's the rent?"

"Ah, nothing."

"What do you mean, nothing?" I asked.

"Just that. Bring six bottles of poison and the space is yours."

"Can we agree on something a little more specific? Say twenty roubles? Would that suit you?"

The owner fell to thought:

"How much is that?"

"I just said – twenty roubles."

"And converted to brew? At rouble four apiece?"

"Nineteen bottles of 'Fortified Rosé'. A pack of 'Belomor' smokes. Two boxes of matches," spat out Tolik.

"And two roubles for moving expenses," concluded Mikhail Ivanych.

I took out the money.

"Do you care to examine the toilet?"

"Another time," I said. "Then we've agreed? Where do you keep the key?"

"There's no key," said Mikhail Ivanych. "It got lost. Don't go, we'll make a run."

"I've got some business at the tourist centre. Next time..."

"As you wish. I'll stop by the centre this evening. I gotta give Lizka a kick in the butt."

"Who's Lizka?" I asked.

"She's my woman. Wife, I mean. Works as a housekeeper at the centre. We be broken up."

"So then why are you going to beat her?"

"Whatsa? Hanging her's too good, but a mess to get into. They wanted to take away my gun, something about me threatening to shoot 'er... I thought you were here about the gun..."

"A waste of ammo," threw in Tolik.

"You don't say," agreed Mikhail Ivanych. "I can snuff 'er with my bare hands, if need be... Last winter I bump into her, this and that, it's all friendly, and she screams: 'Oh, Misha, dearest, I don't want to, let me go...' Major Jafarov summons me in and says, 'Your name?' And I say, 'Dick on a stick.'

"I got me fifteen days in the clink, without smokes, without nothing... Like I give a shit... Just kicking back... Lizka wrote to the prosecutor, something about puttin' me away or I'll kill 'er... But what's the point in that?"

"You won't hear the end of it," agreed Tolik. And added:

"Let's get going! Or they'll close the shop..."

And the friends set off for the housing development, resilient, repulsive and aggressive, like weeds.

I stayed in the library till closing.

It took me three days to prepare for the tour. Galina introduced me to the two guides she thought were the best. I covered the Preserve with them, paying attention and taking a few notes.

The Preserve consisted of three memorial sites: Pushkin's house and estate in Mikhailovskoye; Trigorskoye, where the poet's friends lived and where he visited nearly every day; and finally the monastery with the Pushkin-Hannibal burial plot.

The tour of Mikhailovskoye was made up of several parts. The history of the estate. The poet's second exile. Arina Rodionovna, his nanny. The Pushkin family. Friends who visited the poet in exile. The Decembrist uprising.* And Pushkin's study, with a brief overview of his work.

I found the curator of the museum and introduced myself. Victoria Albertovna looked about forty. A long flouncy skirt, bleached locks, an intaglio and an umbrella – a pretentious painting by Benois.* This style of the dwindling provincial nobility was visibly and deliberately cultivated here. Its characteristic details manifested themselves in each of the museum's

local historians. One would wrap herself tightly in a fantasti-
cally oversized gypsy shawl. Another had an exquisite straw
hat dangling at the back. And the third got stuck with a silly
fan made of feathers.

Victoria Albertovna chatted with me, smiling distrustfully. I
started to get used to that. Everyone in service of the Pushkin
cult was surprisingly begrudging. Pushkin was their collective
property, their adored lover, their tenderly revered child. Any
encroachment on this personal deity irritated them. They were
hasty to prove my ignorance, cynicism and greed.

"Why have you come here?" asked the curator.

"For the rich pickings," I said.

Victoria Albertovna nearly fainted.

"I'm sorry, I was joking."

"Your jokes here are entirely inappropriate."

"I agree. May I ask you one question? Which of the museum's
objects are authentic?"

"Is that important?"

"I think so, yes. After all, it's a museum, not the theatre."

"Everything here is authentic. The river, the hills, the trees
– they are all Pushkin's contemporaries, his companions and
friends. The wondrous nature of these parts…"

"I was asking about objects in the museum," I interrupted.
"The guidebook is evasive about most of them: 'China discovered on the estate…'"

"What specifically are you interested in? What would you
like to see?"

"I don't know, personal effects, if such exist…"

"To whom are you addressing your grievances?"

"What grievances?! And certainly not to you! I was only asking..."

"Pushkin's personal effects? The museum was created decades after his death..."

"And that," I said, "is how it always happens. First they drive the man into the ground and then begin looking for his personal effects. That's how it was with Dostoevsky, that's how it was with Yesenin, and that's how it'll be with Pasternak.* When they come to their senses, they'll start looking for Solzhenitsyn's* personal effects..."

"But we are trying to recreate the colour, the atmosphere," said the curator.

"I see. The bookcase, is it real?"

"At the very least it's from that period."

"And the portrait of Byron?"

"That's real," beamed Victoria Albertovna. "It was given to the Vulfs... There is an inscription... By the by, you're quite pernickety. Personal effects, personal effects... It strikes me as an unhealthy interest..."

I felt like a burglar, caught in someone else's apartment.

"Well, what kind of a museum," I said, "is without it – without the unhealthy interest? A healthy interest is reserved strictly for bacon..."

"Is nature not enough for you? Is it not enough that he wandered around this hillside? Swam in this river? Delighted in these scenic views..."

Why am I bothering her, I thought.

"I see," I said. "Thank you, Vika."

Suddenly she bent down, plucked up some weed, pointedly slapped my face with it and let out a short nervous laugh before walking off, gathering her maxiskirt with flounces.

I joined a group headed for Trigorskoye.

To my surprise, I liked the estate curators, a husband and wife. Being married, they could afford the luxury of being friendly. Polina Fyodorovna appeared to be bossy, energetic and a little conceited. Kolya looked like a bemused slouch and kept to the background.

Trigorskoye was in the middle of nowhere and the management rarely came to visit. The exhibition's layout was beautiful and logical. Pushkin as a youth, charming young ladies in love, an atmosphere of elegant summer romance...

I walked around the park and then down to the river. It was green with upside-down trees. Delicate clouds floated by.

I had an urge to take a dip, but a tour bus had pulled up just then.

I went to the Svyatogorsky Monastery. Old ladies were selling flowers by the gate. I bought a bunch of tulips and walked up to the grave. Tourists were taking photographs by the barrier. Their smiling faces were repugnant. Two sad saps with easels arranged themselves nearby.

I laid down the flowers at the grave and left. I needed to see the layout of the Uspensky Monastery. An echo rolled through the cool stone alcoves. Pigeons slumbered under the domes. The cathedral was real, substantial and graceful. A cracked bell glimmered from the corner of the central chamber. One tourist drummed noisily on it with a key.

In the southern chapel I saw the famous drawing by Bruni.* Also in there glared Pushkin's white death mask. Two enormous paintings reproduced the secret removal and funeral. Alexander Turgenev* looked like a matron...

A group of tourists entered. I went to the exit. I could hear from the back:

"Cultural history knows no other event as tragic... Tsarist rule carried out by the hand of a high-society rascal..."

And so I settled in at Mikhail Ivanych's. He drank without pause. He drank to the point of amazement, paralysis and delirium. Moreover, his delirium expressed itself strictly in obscenities. He swore with the same feeling a dignified older man might have while softly humming a tune – in other words, to himself, without any expectation of approval or protest.

I had seen him sober twice. On these paradoxical days, Mikhail Ivanych had the TV and radio going simultaneously. He would lie down on the bed in his trousers, pull out a box marked "Fairy Cake" and read out loud postcards received over the course of his life. He read and expounded:

"*Hello Godfather!...* Well, hello, hello, you ovine spermatoid... *I'd like to wish you success at work...* He'd like to wish me success... Well, fuck your mama in the ear! *Always yours, Radik...* Always yours, always yours... The hell I need you for?"

Mikhail Ivanych was not liked in the village. People envied him. I'd drink, too, they thought. I'd drink and how, my friends! I'd drink myself into a motherfuckin' grave, I would!

But I got a household to run... What's he got? Mikhail Ivanych had no household. Just the two bony dogs that occasionally disappeared for long stretches of time, a scraggy apple tree and a patch of spring onions.

One rainy evening he and I got talking:

"Misha, did you love your wife?"

"Whatsa?! My wife?! As in my woman?! Lizka, you mean?" Mikhail Ivanych was startled.

"Liza. Yelizaveta Prokhorovna."

"Why do I need to love 'er? Just grab her by the thing and off you go..."

"But what attracted you to her?"

Mikhail Ivanych fell silent for a long time.

"She slept tidy," he said. "Quiet as a caterpillar..."

I got my milk from the neighbours, the Nikitins. They lived respectably. A television set, Kramskoy's *Portrait of a Woman* on the wall..." The master of the house ran errands from five o'clock in the morning. He would fix the fence, potter around in the garden... One time I see he's got a heifer strung up by the legs. Skinning it. The blade gleamed clearest white and was covered in blood...

Mikhail Ivanych held the Nikitins in contempt. As they did him, naturally.

"Still drinking?" enquired Nadezhda Fyodorovna, mixing chicken feed in the pail.

"I saw him at the centre," said Nikitin, wielding a jointer plane. "Laced since the morning."

I didn't want to encourage them.

"But he is kind."

"Kind," agreed Nikitin. "Nearly killed his wife with a knife. Set all 'er dresses ablaze. The little ones running around in canvas shoes in winter... But yes, other than that he's kind..."

"Misha is a reckless man, I understand, but he is also kind and noble at heart..."

It's true there was something aristocratic about Mikhail Ivanych. He didn't return empty bottles, for example; he threw them away.

"I'd feel ashamed," he'd say. "How could I, like a beggar?"

One day he woke up feeling poorly and complained:

"I've got the shakes all over."

I gave him a rouble. At lunchtime I asked:

"How goes it, feeling any better?"

"Whatsa?"

"Did you have a pick-me-up?"

"Huh! It went down like water on a hot pan, it sizzled!"

In the evening he was in pain again.

"I'll go see Nikitin. Maybe he'll gimme a rouble or just pour some..."

I stepped onto the porch and was witness to this conversation:

"Hey, neighbour, you scrud, gimme a fiver."

"You owe me since Intercession."*

"I'll pay you back."

"We'll talk when you do."

"You'll get it when I get paid."

"Get paid?! You got booted for cause ages ago."

"Fuck 'em and the horse they rode in on! Gimme a fiver

anyway. Do it on principle, for Christ's sake! Show them our Soviet character!"

"Don't tell me, for vodka?"

"Whatsa? I got business…"

"A parasite like you? What kinda business?"

Mikhail Ivanych found it hard to lie; he was weak.

"I need a drink," he said.

"I won't give it to you. Be mad, if you want, but I won't give it you!"

"But I'll pay you back, from my wages."

"No."

And to end the conversation Nikitin went back into the house, slamming the heavy door with the blue mailbox.

"You just wait, neighbour," fumed Mikhail Ivanych. "You wait! You're gonna get yours! That's right! You'll remember this conversation!"

There was no sound in response. Chickens maundered about. Golden braids of onions hung above the porch…

"I'll make your life hell! I'll…"

Red-faced and dishevelled, Mikhail Ivanych bellowed:

"Have you forgot?! Have you forgot everything, you snake? Clean forgot it?!"

"What'd I forget?" Nikitin leant out.

"If you forgot, we'll remind you!"

"What'd I forget, eh?"

"We remember everything! We remember 1917! We whatchamacallit… We dispossessed you, you scummy scrud! We'll dispossess your whole Party lot! We'll ship you off to the

Cheka... Like Daddy Makhno*... There they'll show you..."
And after a short pause:
"Hey neighbour, lend me a fiver... All right, a trey... I'm begging you, for the love of Christ... you larder bitch!"

Finally I mustered up the courage to start work. I was assigned a group of tourists from the Baltics. These were reserved, disciplined people who listened contentedly and did not ask questions. I tried to be brief and was not entirely sure I was being understood.

Later I would be given a full overview. Tourists from Riga are the best-mannered. Whatever you say, they smile and nod in agreement. If they do ask questions, then they're always on the practical side: how many serfs did Pushkin own? What was the revenue from Mikhailovskoye? What was the total cost of renovations to the manor house?

The Caucasians behaved differently. Generally, they didn't listen at all. They talked among themselves and laughed loudly. On the drive to Trigorskoye they lovingly gazed at the sheep. Evidently they were able to identify their potential as kebabs. And if they asked questions, it was always something entirely unexpected. For instance: "What was the duel between Pushkin and Lermontov about?"*

And as for our compatriots, they must be differentiated. Labourers needed a concise and simple account. Office workers required some concentration; some of them were quite erudite. They've read a lot of Pikul, Rozhdestvensky, Meylakh... Gleaned ludicrous facts from Novikov...*

The intelligentsia were the most contentious and cunning. They would do their homework in preparation for their touristic voyage. Some random fact would get stuck in their memory. A distant relative. A curious escapade, rejoinder, incident... An inconsequential reference... And so on.

On my third day of work a woman with glasses asked me: "When was Benckendorff* born?"

"In the Seventies," I replied.

Uncertainty was discernible in my answer.

"And more precisely?" she pressed.

"Unfortunately," I said, "I've forgotten."

And I thought to myself, why am I lying? Why not simply admit: "Who the hell knows?" There's no great thrill in Benckendorff's coming into the world.

"Alexander Christopherovich Benckendorff," the woman reproached, "was born in 1784. In June, incidentally..."

I nodded, letting her know that I valued this information.

From that moment on an ironic smile did not leave her. As if my indifference towards Benckendorff betrayed my complete poverty of spirit...

And so I started working. The methodologists usually don't listen to your first tour. They give you a chance to feel your way around, to get comfortable. And that is what saved me, because this is what happened.

I successfully navigated through the vestibule. Pointed out the drawing by the land surveyor Ivanov. Talked about Pushkin's first exile. Then the second. I made my way to Arina

Rodionovna's room: "The only person who was truly close to the poet was his nanny, a serf..." It was all going smoothly. "She was both forgiving and curmudgeonly, naively religious and exceptionally businesslike..." Bas-relief by Seryakov...* "She was offered freedom, but refused it..."

And finally:

"The poet often turned to the nanny in verse. For instance, everyone knows these heartfelt lines..."

For a second I lost my train of thought, and shuddered at the sound of my own voice:

"Still around, old dear? How are you keeping?

I too am around. Hello to you!

May that magic twilight ever be streaming

Over your cottage as it used to do."

I was mortified. Any moment someone would cry out:

"You fool and ignoramus! This is Yesenin – 'A Letter to Mother'..."

I continued reciting, feverishly trying to come up with something to say.

"Yes, comrades, you are absolutely right. Of course this is Yesenin. Yes, his 'Letter to Mother'. But please note just how close Pushkin's intonation is to the lyricism of Sergei Yesenin. How organically it is realized in Yesenin's poetics..." And so on.

I continued reciting. Somewhere at the end a Finnish knife flashed ominously...* "Blah-blah-blah in a drunken tavern scuffle, blah-blah-blah a Finnish knife into my chest..." An inch away from this shining, menacing blade I was able to stop. I waited for a storm after the ensuing silence. But everyone was quiet. Their faces appeared impassioned and stern. Only one elderly tourist pronounced weightily:

"Yeah, there were men..."

In the next room I attributed *Mnemosyne* to Delvig.* Then called Sergei Lvovich "Sergei Alexandrovich".* (Evidently, Yesenin had firmly occupied my subconscious.) But these were mere trifles. And I won't even mention the three dubious literary speculations.

At Trigorskoye and in the monastery the tour went well. I had to think up logical transitions between the rooms. Find the so-called links. For a long time, I had difficulty with one particular passage – between Zizi's room and the parlour. Finally I came up with this lacklustre tie-in and used it unfalteringly:

"My friends! I see it's a little tight in here. Let's move into the next room!"

At the same time, I would listen to other tours and in each find something interesting for myself. I befriended guides from Leningrad who for many years had spent their summers in the Preserve.

One of them was Volodya Mitrofanov. He was the one who sold me on the idea and came here right in my footsteps. More must be said about this man.

During his school years, Mitrofanov was known for his "photographic memory", as they say. He would memorize entire chapters from textbooks with ease. He was presented as a miracle child. What's more, God had blessed him with an unquenchable thirst for knowledge. His was a combination of limitless curiosity and phenomenal memory. A brilliant career in the sciences awaited him.

Everything interested Mitrofanov: biology, geography, field theory, ventriloquism, stamp-collecting, Suprematism,* the fundamentals of animal training... He read three serious books a day. He graduated from school triumphantly and was accepted to the philology department at the university without any effort.

His professors were stumped: Mitrofanov knew absolutely everything and demanded new information. For his benefit, distinguished scientists spent days in libraries, poring over long-forgotten theories and science disciplines. Concurrently, Mitrofanov attended lectures on law, biology and chemistry.

The combination of a unique memory and an immeasurable thirst for knowledge worked wonders. But a shocking circumstance came to light: Mitrofanov's personality was completely and fully exhausted by these qualities. He possessed no other attributes. He was born a genius of pure learning.

His first paper was left unfinished. Or rather, he put down only the first sentence. Actually, the beginning of the first sentence. Specifically: "As we all know..." At this juncture, the brilliantly conceived work was cut short.

Mitrofanov grew into a fantastic sloth, if one can call lazy a man who had read ten thousand books.

Mitrofanov did not wash his face, did not shave and did not attend Communal Work Saturdays. He did not repay his debts and did not lace his boots. He was too lazy to put on a hat. He simply laid it on top of his head.

He failed to appear for mandatory work placement at a

collective farm. He just didn't show up, without explanation.

The university expelled Mitrofanov. His friends tried to find him a job. For a short while, he was a personal secretary to the academic Firsov. At first everything was perfect. Mitrofanov spent hours at the Academy of Sciences library, gathering research material for Firsov. And he readily shared the information already stored in his memory. The elderly scholar came to life. He offered Volodya a partnership in the development of his diatonal geomorphogenetic theory (or something like that). The academic said:

"You will do the writing. I am short-sighted."

The next day Mitrofanov was gone. He was too lazy to take notes

For several months he did nothing. He read another three hundred books and learnt two languages: Romanian and Hindi. He ate at his friends' homes, repaying them with brilliant, wide-ranging lectures. People gave him their old clothes.

Friends tried to get him a job at the Lenfilm Studios. What's more, a special position was created just for him: Consultant on All Matters. This was a rare stroke of luck. Mitrofanov was familiar with the costumes and customs of every era. He knew the fauna of every corner of the globe and the tiniest details in the flow of prehistoric events. He remembered paradoxical statements made by secondary government officials, the number of buttons on Talleyrand's waistcoat and the name of Lomonosov's wife...*

Mitrofanov failed to fill out the application form. Even its sections that read "underline where applicable". He was lazy...

Finally, friends got him a job as a watchman at a movie theatre. It was a night job, so you could sleep if you wanted, or read, or think, if you were so inclined. Mitrofanov had but a single responsibility – after midnight he had to flip on some sort of switch. And he'd forget to do it. Or was too lazy. He got fired...

Later on, we were disheartened to learn that Mitrofanov wasn't simply a slacker. He was diagnosed with a rare clinical condition – aboulia, or total atrophy of will.

He was a phenomenon that belonged to the vegetable kingdom, a bright, fanciful flower. A chrysanthemum cannot hoe its own soil and water itself.

And then Mitrofanov heard about Pushkin Hills. He came, looked around and ascertained that this was the only institution where he could be useful.

What's expected of a tour guide? A vivid and dramatic story, and nothing more.

And Mitrofanov knew how to tell a story. His tours were full of surprising references, dazzling suppositions, rare archival notes and quotations in six languages.

His tours were twice longer than the average. At times, tourists fainted from the strain.

There were some complications, of course: Mitrofanov was reluctant to climb Savkin Hill. The tourists struggled to the top while Mitrofanov stood at the foot of the knoll, articulating:

"As it has for so many years, this large green mound rises above the river Sorot. The remarkable symmetry of its form points to its artificial origins. When it comes to the etymology of the name *Sorot*, it is rather curious, even if not entirely decorous..."

Once the tourists laid out a fake leather coat and hauled Mitrofanov up the hill, while he continued broadcasting with a satisfied smile:

"Legend has it that one of the Voronich monasteries stood on this site..."

He was valued at the Preserve...

A no less colourful personality was Stasik Pototsky. He was born in Cheboksary and until the age of sixteen did not stand out. He played hockey without giving a thought to serious matters. Then finally he turned up in Leningrad with a delegation of young athletes.

On the very first day, he lost his virginity to a floor monitor at the Hotel Sokol. He was lucky – she was old and affectionate. She treated the junior to Alabashly wine and whispered to her drunk and lovesick boy:

"Look at you! So little yet so spirited!"

Pototsky quickly came to realize that there were two things on this earth worth living for – wine and women. The rest did not deserve his attention. But women and wine cost money. Therefore, you had to know how to earn it. Preferably without much effort and without ending up in jail.

He decided to become a writer of best-sellers. He read twelve contemporary novels and grew confident that he could do no worse. And so he bought a calico notebook, a ballpoint pen and a refill.

His first composition was published in *Youth Magazine*. The story was titled 'The Victory of Shurka Chemodanov'. A young hockey player, Chemodanov, becomes full of himself and quits school. Then he comes to his senses, turns into a model student and an even better hockey player. The piece ended like this:

"'The most important thing, Shurka, is being a human being,' said Lukyanych, and walked away. For a long, long time, Shurka's eyes followed him…"

The story was extraordinarily unremarkable. Hundreds just like it graced the pages of youth magazines. The editors were forgiving towards Pototsky. Apparently he deserved a break, as a provincial author.

Within a year, he succeeded in publishing seven short stories and a novella. His creations were banal, ideologically sound and dull. A recognizable thread ran through all of them. A reliable armour of literary conventionality protected them from censorship. They sounded convincing, like quotations. The most exciting things about them were syntax errors and misprints:

"Misha excepted that he had finally turned thirteen…" (From the story 'Misha's Woe'.)

"'May he rest in piece!' Odintsov concluded his speech…" (From the story 'The Smoke Rises Skyward'.)

"'Don't throw a wench in the works,' threatened Lepko…" (From the novel *Seagulls Fly to the Horizon*.)

Later Pototsky would say to me:

"I'm a fuckin' writer, sort of like Chekhov. Chekhov was absolutely right. You can write a story just about anything. There's no shortage of subject matter. Take any profession. Say a doctor. And here you have it: a fuckin' surgeon goes to operate and recognizes his patient as the man who slept with his wife. The surgeon is faced with a moral fuckin' dilemma – to save the man or cut off his... No, that's too much, that's fuckin' overkill. Bottom line, the surgeon is hesitant. Then he picks up a scalpel and performs a miracle. The fuckin' end goes something like this: 'For a long, long time the nurse's gaze followed him...' Or take the sea, for example," Pototsky went on, "Nothing to it... A sailor retires and leaves his beloved fuckin' ship. His friends, his past, his youth are all left behind. He goes for a walk along the Fontanka River, looking forlorn. And he spots a fuckin' drowning boy. Without a second thought the sailor leaps into the icy vortex. Risking his life, he saves the kid. The end goes like this: 'Vitya will never forget this hand. Large, calloused, with a light-blue anchor on the wrist...' Meaning – a sailor will always be a sailor, even if he is fuckin' retired..."

Pototsky would complete a story a day. He published a book. It was called *Dark Roads to Happiness*. It received kind reviews that gently pointed out the author's backwater origins.

Stasik decided to leave Cheboksary. He wanted to spread his wings, so he moved to Leningrad and became very fond of the Europa restaurant and two models.

In Leningrad, his stories were received coolly. The standards there were a little higher. A complete absence of talent did not pay, while its presence made people nervous. Genius instilled fear. The most bankable were "obvious literary abilities". Pototsky had no obvious abilities. Something glimmered in his compositions, slipped through, flickered. An accidental phrase, an unexpected remark... "Opaline bulb of garlic." "A stewardess on paraffin legs." But no obvious abilities.

They stopped publishing him. What was forgiven a provincial novice affronted in a cosmopolitan writer. Stasik started to drink, and not in Europa but in artists' basements. And not with models, but with the floor-monitor friend. (She now sold fruit from a stall.)

He drank for four years. Did a year for vagrancy. The floor-monitor friend (now a worker in the food industry) left him. He may have given her a beating, or stolen from her...

His clothes turned into rags. Friends ceased lending him money and refrained from giving him cast-off slacks. The militia threatened to throw him back in jail for violating the residency rules. Someone put him on to Pushkin Hills. This lifted his spirits. Stasik prepared, began giving tours. And he wasn't bad. His trump card was his confiding intimacy:

"Pushkin's personal tragedy causes us heartache even to this day..."

Pototsky embellished his monologues with fantastic detail, acted out the duel scene in character, and once even fell on the grass. He would conclude the tour with a mysterious metaphysical contrivance:

"Finally, after a long and agonizing illness, Russia's great citizen had succumbed, but d'Anthès is still alive, comrades..."*

Every now and again he would go on a binge, neglecting his job, bumming some change in front of a local watering hole, hunting for empty bottles in the bushes and sleeping on the cracked gravestone of Alexei Nikolayevich Vulf.

Whenever Captain Shatko of the militia ran into him, he'd

say reproachfully:

"Pototsky, your appearance disturbs the harmony of these parts."

Then Pototsky came up with a new gimmick. He would stroll through the monastery on the trail of the next group. Lie in wait by the grave until the end of the tour. Call the group leader to the side and whisper:

"*Antra noo!* Between us! Pull thirty copecks each and I'll show you the true grave of Pushkin that the Bolsheviks are hiding from the people!"

He then would lead the group into the woods, pointing to a nondescript mound. Occasionally some stickler would ask:

"But why would they conceal the real grave?"

"Why?" Pototsky would flash a sardonic smile. "You want to know why? Comrades, this compatriot is asking why?"

"I see, I see," the tourist would mutter.

On the day I arrived, Stasik was worn out after a week-long binge. He wangled a rouble from me and a pair of brown sandals with perforations. Then he shared a dramatic story:

"I nearly made a fortune, man. I came up with this exceptional financial trick. Listen: I meet some sucker. He's got a car, some cash, some other fuckin' shit. We take one, note, just one broad and drive out into the great outdoors. There we both check in—"

"I don't understand."

"Take turns with her. The next morning I show up at his place, screaming 'Man, my dick's dripping.' He panics, so I say: 'I can be of fuckin' service, for twenty-five bills.' The fool jumps for joy. I fill a syringe with tap water and give us both a shot in the derrière. The chump happily tosses me the bills and we part friends. The broad gets some stockings for seven roubles. That's eighteen roubs of pure profit. It was brilliant. Operation – Clap Trap. And fuckin' hell, it fell through..."

"Why?"

"At first everything went smoothly. The chump was wild about me. We picked up some cognac, sandwiches. I enlisted cross-eyed Milka who works at the Cavalier, and we took off for the great fuckin' outdoors. We booze it up, get down to business and guess what? The next morning, the sap shows up at my place, screaming, 'Fuck, my pecker's dripping,' gets in his fuckin' car and takes off. I rush to the clinic to find Fima. This and that, I say. And Fima goes: 'Twenty-five roubles!'... Dear God, who's got that kind of cash?! I had to run around all over Pskov and the city limits and barely scraped it together... Eleven days I stayed sober and then I fuckin' broke fast. What about you, how are you on the subject?"

"You mean the great outdoors?"

"I mean a drink."

I waved my arms in protest. A start is all I need. It's stopping that I never learnt. A dump truck without brakes.

Stas flipped a rouble coin in his palm and left...

"Your evaluation is tomorrow," said Galina.

"So soon?"

"I think you're ready. Why put it off?"

At first I was nervous, noticing Victoria Albertovna among the tourists. Vika was smiling, kindly or perhaps ironically.

Gradually I became bolder. The group was demanding – voluntary-army activists from Torzhok – they kept asking questions.

"This," I say, "is the famous portrait by Kiprensky... commissioned by Delvig... sublime treatment... hints of romantic embellishment... 'I see myself as if in a looking glass...'* Bought by Pushkin for the Baron's widow..."

"When? What year?"

"I think in 1830."

"For how much?"

"What's the difference?!" I exploded.

Vika was trying to help me, silently moving her lips.

We entered the study. I pointed out the portrait of Byron, the cane, the bookcase... I moved on to the work... "Intense period... Articles... Draft of the magazine...", "*Godunov*", "*Gypsies*"... The library... "I shall soon die completely, but if you love my shadow..."* And so on.

Suddenly I hear:

"Are the pistols real?"

"An original duelling set from Le Page."

The same voice:

"Le Page? I though they were Pushkin's."

I explained:

"The pistols are from the same period. Made by the famous gunsmith Le Page. Pushkin knew and appreciated good firearms. He owned the same pistols..."

"What about the calibre?"

"What *about* the calibre?"

"I am interested in the calibre."

"The calibre," I said, "is just right."

"Very good." The tourist unexpectedly submitted.

While my group looked at the nanny's home, Victoria Albertovna whispered:

"Your delivery is very good, very natural... You have your own personal point of view. But never... I am simply horrified... You called Pushkin a crazed ape..."

"That's not entirely true."

"I beg you – a little more restraint."

"I will try."

"But overall it's not bad..."

I began giving tours regularly. Sometimes two in one shift. Evidently they liked me. If we had cultural leaders, teachers or the intelligentsia in – they got me. Something in my tours stood out. For example, my "easy-going manner of presentation", according to the curator at Trigorskoye. This was, of course, largely due to my acting ability. Even though I had memorized the entire text after approximately five days, I had no trouble simulating emotional improvisation. I artfully stammered as if searching for words, deliberately slipped up, waved my arms, embellishing my carefully rehearsed impromptu remarks with aphorisms from Gukovsky and Shchegolev.* The more I got to know Pushkin, the less I felt like talking about him. Especially at this embarrassing level. I performed my role mechanically and was well remunerated for it. (A full tour was about eight roubles.)

I found a dozen rare books about Pushkin in the local library.

I also reread everything he wrote. What intrigued me most about Pushkin was his Olympian detachment. His willingness to accept and express any point of view. His invariable striving for the highest, utmost objectivity. Like the moon, illuminating the way for prey and predator both.

Not a monarchist, not a conspirator and not a Christian – he was only a poet, a genius, and he felt compassion for the cycle of life as a whole.

His literature is above morality. It transcends morality and even takes its place. His literature is akin to prayer, to nature… But then I'm not a critic…

My working day began at nine in the morning. We sat at the office, waiting for clients. The conversation was about Pushkin and about tourists. More often about tourists, about their inconceivable ignorance.

"Can you imagine, he asked me, 'Who is Boris Godunov?'"

Personally, I did not feel annoyed in similar situations. Or rather, I did, but I suppressed it. The tourists came here to relax. Their union committee forced these cheap destinations on them. By and large, these people were indifferent towards poetry. To them, Pushkin was a symbol of culture. What was important to them was the sensation that they were there. To tick a mental box. To sign the book of spirituality…

It was my responsibility to bring them this happiness without tiring them out. And to receive seven roubles sixty and a touching mention in the guestbook:

"Pushkin came alive thanks to such-and-such tour guide and his humble insight."

My days were all the same. The tours were over at two. I ate lunch at The Seashore and went home. Several times Mitrofanov and Pototsky invited me to join them for a drink. I turned them down. This did not take any effort on my part. I can easily refuse the first drink. It's the stopping that I haven't learnt. The motor is good but the brakes fail me...

I did not write to my wife and daughter. There was no point. I thought I'd wait and see what happened.

In short, my life stabilized somewhat. I tried to think less about abstract topics. The cause of my unhappiness lay outside my field of vision. It was somewhere behind me. And I was relatively calm if I wasn't looking back. Best not to look back.

In the meantime, I read Likhonosov.* Of course he is a good writer – talented, colourful, fluid. He recreates direct speech brilliantly. (Tolstoy should get such a compliment!) And yet at the heart of it is a hopeless, depressing and nagging feeling. A tedious and exhausted motif: "Where are you, Russia? Where did everything go? Where are the folk verses, the embroidered towels, the fancy headdresses? Where is the hospitality, bravery and the grand scale? Where are the samovars, icons, ascetics and holy fools? Where are the sturgeon and carp, the honey and caviar? Where are the regular horses, God damn it? Where is the chaste feeling of modesty?"

They are racking their brains:

"Where are you, Russia? Where did you disappear? Who ruined you?"

Who, who... Everyone knows who... There's no need to rack your brain...

My relationship with Mikhail Ivanych was simple and consistent. In the beginning, he often came to see me, pulling out bottles from his pockets. I would wave my arms in protest. He drank directly from the bottle, muttering in a steady stream. It was with some difficulty that I caught the gist of his extensive monologues.

What's more, Misha's speech was organized in a remarkable way. Only nouns and verbs were pronounced with clarity and dependability. Mostly in inappropriate combinations. All secondary parts of speech Mikhail Ivanych used at his sole discretion. Whichever ones happened to turn up. Never mind the prepositions, particles and conjunctions. He created them as he went along. His speech was not unlike classical music, abstract art or the song of a goldfinch. Emotions clearly prevailed over meaning.

Let's imagine I said:

"Misha, perhaps you should lay off the sauce, if only for a little while."

In response I'd hear:

"Tha' maggot-faggot, God knows wha'... Gets a fiver in the morning an' shoot to the piss factory... Advance is on deposit... How'sa imma quit?... Whatsa smart in'at?... Where'sa spirit rise."

Misha's overtures were reminiscent of the Remizov school of writing.*

He called gossipy women prattletraps. Bad housewives – majordodos. Unfaithful women – peter-cheetahs. Beer and vodka – sledgehammer, poison and kerosene. And the young generation – pussberries...

"Copper-trouble pussberries be hullabaplonking an' God knows whatsa at the centre..."

Meaning – the young generation, the underage bums are causing trouble and God knows what...

Our relationship was clearly defined. Misha would bring me onions, sour cream, mushrooms and potatoes from his mother-in-law. And he vehemently refused to take money. I, in turn, gave him a rouble every morning for wine. And kept him from trying to shoot his wife, Liza. Sometimes putting my own life in danger.

So we were even.

I never did figure out what sort of man he was. He seemed absurd, kind and inept. Once he strung up two cats on a rowan tree, making the nooses with a fishing line.

"Breeding shebangers," he said, "catervaulting about..."

Once I accidentally bolted the door from the inside and he sat on the porch till morning, afraid to wake me up...

Misha was absurd in both his kindness and his anger. He reviled the authorities to their faces, but tipped his hat when passing a portrait of Friedrich Engels. He cursed the Rhodesian dictator, Ian Smith, relentlessly, but loved and respected the barmaid at a local dive who invariably short-changed him:

"That's the way things are. Order is order!"

His worst insult went something like this:

"You're bending over for the capitalists!"

Once officer Doveyko took a German bayonet away from a very drunken Misha.

"Serving the capitalists, you scum!" Mikhail Ivanych raged.

One time when he was out, his wife and mother-in-law made off with his radio.

"They'll still get no thanks from the capitalists," assured Mikhail Ivanych.

Only about twice did he and I have a conversation. I remember Misha saying (the text has been slightly cleaned up):

"I was a pup when the Germans installed here. Truth be told, they did no harm. They took the chickens, old man Timokha's pig, but they did no harm... And they hadn't laid a finger on the dames. The skirts took offence, even... My old man cooked his own brew and traded it for food with the Nazis... They did fix the Yids and the Gypsies, though..."

"You mean, shot them?"

"Got rid of 'em for good. Order is order..."

"And you say they did no harm."

"I swear to God, they done no harm. The Yids and the Gypsies – that's the nature of things..."

"What have the Jews ever done to you?"

"I got respect for the Jews. I'd trade a dozen Ukey bums for one Jew. But Gypsies, I'd strangle the lot of 'em with my bare hands."

"Why?"

"Whadda you mean why? You kidding?! A Gypsy's a Gypsy!"

In July I began to write. These were odd sketches, dialogues, a search for the right tone. Something like a synopsis with vaguely outlined figures and themes. Tragic love, debts, marriage, writing, conflict with the authorities. Plus, as Dostoevsky used to say, a hint of greater meaning.

I thought this enterprise would erase my miseries. This had happened before, when I was starting out in my literary pursuits. I think it's called sublimation. When you try to make literature take responsibility for your sins. A man writes *King Lear* and for the whole year he need not raise his sword...

Soon I sent my wife seventeen roubles. And bought myself a shirt – for me, an action without precedent.

There were rumours about some publications in the West. I tried not to think about it. After all, what do I care about what goes on on the other side? And that's exactly what I'll say, if they send for me...

I also mailed out a few IOUs to the effect that I'm working, will pay you back soon, apologies...

All my creditors reacted magnanimously: there's no rush, I'm not pressed for money, pay me back when you can...

In short, life became balanced. It started to seem more sensible, more logical. After all, nightmares and hopelessness are not the worst things... The worst thing is chaos...

All it takes is a week without vodka and the fog clears. Life acquires a relatively sharp outline. Even our problems seem like natural phenomena.

I was afraid to ruin this fragile balance – I became rude when offered a drink, irritable if girls at the main office tried to start a conversation...

Pototsky said:

"Boris sober and Boris drunk are such different people, they've never even met."

And yet I knew that this couldn't continue for ever. You cannot walk away from life's problems... Weak men endure life; courageous ones master it... If you live wrongly, sooner or later something will happen...

Morning. Milk with a bluish skin. Dogs barking, buckets jangling...

Misha's hungover voice from behind the wall:

"Sonny, throw me a singleton!"

I emptied out my leftover change and fed the dogs.

Beyond the hill at the tourist centre the radiogram was playing. Jackdaws flew through the clear skies. Fog spread over the marsh, at the foot of the mountain. Sheep reposed in grey clumps on the green grass.

I walked through the field to the tourist centre. Yellow sand stuck to my boots, wet from the morning dew. The air from the grove carried chill and smoke.

Tourists sat under the windows of the main office. On a bench, covered with newspaper, sprawled Mitrofanov. Even asleep he was perceptibly lazy...

I walked up the steps. The tour guides huddled in the small hall. Someone said hello. Someone asked for a light. Dima Baranov said: "What's the matter with you?"

Under a dreadful, horrific, repellent painting by the local artist Shchukin (top hat, horse, genius, endless horizon) stood my wife, smiling...

At that moment my miserable well-being came to an end. I knew what lay ahead. I remembered our last conversation...

We were divorced a year and a half ago. This elegant modern divorce felt a little like an armistice. An armistice that didn't always end with a flash of rockets...

I remember when Justice of the Peace Chikvaidze asked my wife:

"Do you wish to claim a part of the property?"

"No," replied Tatyana.

Then added:

"In the absence of such."

After that we would occasionally meet as old friends, but it seemed phoney and I left for Tallinn.

A year later we met again. Our daughter was sick and Tanya moved in with me. This was no longer about love, this was fate...

We had little money and we fought often. A potful of mutual irritation bubbled quietly over a low flame...

In Tanya's mind, the image of an unrecognized genius was clearly linked to the idea of asceticism. I, to put it mildly, was too sociable.

I said:

"Pushkin chased after women... Dostoevsky indulged in gambling... Yesenin caroused and started fights in restaurants... Vice was just as common to men of genius as virtue..."

"Then you must be at least half genius," my wife would agree, "for you have more than enough vices..."

We continued to balance on the edge of a cliff. They say marriages like this are most enduring.

And yet the friendship was over. You can't say, "Hey, my

dear!" to a woman to whom you have whispered God knows what. It doesn't ring right...

With what did I arrive at my thirtieth birthday, celebrated boisterously at the Dnieper restaurant? I led the life of an independent artist. That is to say I did not hold a regular job and earned money as a journalist and ghostwriter of some generals' memoirs. I had an apartment with windows looking out onto a garbage dump. A writing table, a couch, a set of dumb-bells and a Tonus radiogram. A typewriter, a guitar, a picture of Hemingway and several pipes, kept in a ceramic mug. A lamp, a wardrobe, two chairs of the brontosaurus period, and a cat named Yefim, whom I respected deeply for his tact. Unlike my close friends and acquaintances, he strived to be a human being...

Tanya lived in the next room. Our daughter would get sick with something, then she'd get better, then sick again.

My friend Bernovich always said:

"By the time he is thirty, an artist must have resolved all his problems. Except for one – how to write."

I claimed that fundamental problems were irresolvable. For instance, the conflict between fathers and sons. The struggle between love and duty...

We got our terminology mixed up.

In the end Bernovich would invariably say:

"You are not made for marriage..."

And yet we've been married ten years. Just short of ten years.

Tatyana rose over my life like the dawn's morning light. That is, calmly, beautifully, without encouraging excessive emotions.

Excessive was only her indifference. Her limitless indifference was comparable to a natural phenomenon...

An artist by the name Lobanov was celebrating his hamster's birthday. About a dozen people crammed into the garret with a sloping ceiling. Everyone waited for Tselkov, who didn't show. They sat on the floor even though there were plenty of chairs. By nightfall, table talk had escalated to a dispute with undertones of a fist fight. A man sporting a buzz cut and a sailor's striped jersey was losing his voice, screaming:

"I'll say it one more time, colour is ideological in aspect!"

(It was later discovered that he wasn't an artist at all, but a store clerk from the Apraksin shopping centre.)

This innocent phrase for some reason infuriated one of the guests, a typeface designer. He charged at the store clerk with his fists. But the clerk, like all men with shaved heads, was brawny and acted fast. He immediately removed a false tooth, supported by a pin... swiftly wrapped it in a handkerchief and tucked into his pocket. He then assumed a boxer's stance.

By now the artist had cooled off.

He was eating stuffed fish, exclaiming between bites:

"Fantastic fish! I'd like to have children with her. Three of them."

I noticed Tanya right away. Right away I memorized her face, both apprehensive and indifferent. (In all my years, I have never understood how indifference and alarm can coexist in a woman.)

Her lipstick stood out against her pale face. Her smile was childlike and a little anxious.

Later someone sang, trying hard to imitate a recidivist thief. Someone invited a foreign diplomat, who turned out to be a Greek sailor. The poet Karpovsky told extravagant lies. For example he said that he was booted from the International Pen Club for artistic hooliganism.

I took Tatyana's hand and said:

"Let's get out of here!"

(The best way to overcome inherent insecurity is to act as confidently as you can.)

Tanya acquiesced without hesitation. And not like a conspirator, more like an obedient child, a young lady who willingly does as she's told.

I moved towards the door, flung it open and froze. Glistening before me was a sloping wet roof. The antennas soared black against the pale sky.

Apparently the studio had three doors. One led to the elevator, another to the underbelly of the heating system, and the third to the roof.

I didn't feel like going back. And judging by the rising volume inside, the evening's celebrations were headed for a brawl.

I hesitated for a moment and stepped onto the rumbling roof. Tanya followed me.

"I've been dreaming of romantic surroundings like this for a long time," I said.

A torn shoe lay under my foot. A sad grey cat was poised on the sharp ridge pole.

I asked:

"Have you ever been on a roof before?"

"No, never," replied Tanya.

And added:

"But I have always been terribly envious of Gagarin..."

"There," I said, "is the Kazan Cathedral... Behind it, the Admiralty... And this is the Pushkin Theatre..."

We walked over to the railing. In the distance below, the evening city was abuzz. From above, the street seemed faceless and only the light-filled trams gave it a little life.

"We need to find a way out of here," I said.

"Do you think the fight is over?"

"I doubt it. How did you wind up here? With this set?"

"Through my ex-husband."

"What is he, an artist?"

"Not exactly... He turned out to be a lowlife. And you?"

"What about me?"

"How did you wind up here?"

"Lobanov roped me into it. I bought a painting from him, out of snobbery. Something white... with ears... Like a squid... It's called *Vector of Calm*... Are there talented painters among this lot?"

"Yes. Tselkov, for example."

"Which one was he? The one in jeans?"

"Tselkov is the one who didn't show."

"I see," I said.

"One hanged himself not too long ago. His name was Fish. His nickname. He went and hanged himself."

"Dear God, why? Love affair gone bad?"

"Fish was over thirty. His paintings didn't sell."

"They were good paintings?"

"Not really. He works as a proofreader now."

"Who?" I exclaimed.

"Fish. They managed to save him. A neighbour stopped by for a cigarette."

"We need to find a way out."

Treading lightly, I made it to the small window in the attic. I threw it open and extended my hand to the young woman:

"Be careful!"

Tanya easily slipped through the opening. I followed after her. The attic was dark and dusty. We stepped over pipes wrapped in felt blankets and stooped to avoid clothes lines. We found the backstairs and walked down. Then navigated through the connecting courtyards and happened upon a taxi stand.

It was raining and I thought: here it is, our Petersburg literary tradition. This much vaunted "school" is nothing more than endless descriptions of bad weather. The whole "dull lustre of its style" is just asphalt after the rain…

Then I asked:

"How are your mother and father? They must be worried."

For fifteen years I've been asking pretty women this stupid question. Three out of five say:

"I live alone, so there's no one to worry about."

And that is precisely what I want to hear. An old adage states: it is easier to fight a battle on enemy territory…

"I have no parents," glumly replied Tanya.

I felt embarrassed.

"I am sorry," I said, "it was tactless."

"They live in Yalta," she added. "Father is a local district committee secretary."

A taxi pulled up.

"Where to?" asked the driver without turning around.

"Dzerzhinsky Street, number 8."

The driver shrugged his shoulders in annoyance.

"You could've walked."

"Don't worry, we'll square up," I said.

The driver turned to me, punctuating every word:

"My gratitude, kind sir! We shall never forget your generosity…"

We drove up to Tanya's building. Its brick façade protruded from the general rank by a few feet. Four wide Victorian windows were connected by a railing.

The driver made a U-turn and left, saying:

"*Auf Wiedersehen…*"

The shallow steps led to a heavy, tarpaulin-covered door.

I'd been in this situation a thousand times before and yet I felt nervous. Now she will walk up the steps and I'll hear:

"Thank you for seeing me home…"

You must leave after this. To loiter about the entrance is unseemly. To ask for "a little nightcap" is contemptible!

My friend Bernovich used to say:

"It's a good thing to go when you're invited. It's horrible when you're not invited. But best of all is when you're invited and you don't go…"

Tanya cracked open the door:

"Thank you for the roof!"

"You know," I said, "what I feel bad about? There was a lot

of alcohol left... Back at the studio..."

And, as if unintentionally, I crossed the threshold.

"I have wine," said Tanya. "I hide it from my cousin. He shows up with a bottle and I sneak half of it into the cupboard. He has a bad liver..."

"You've intrigued me," I said.

"I hear you," said Tatyana. "I have an uncle who is a chronic alcoholic..."

We entered the elevator. A small light blinked at every floor. Tanya was looking down at her sandals. An expensive pair, by the way, with the Rochas label...

I could see an obscenity scrawled in chalk behind her. An insult without an addressee. Expression of pure art...

Then we tiptoed very quietly, almost furtively, down the corridor. My sleeves swished against the wallpaper.

"You are huge," whispered Tanya.

"And you," I said, "are observant."

We found ourselves in a surprisingly large room. I saw a clay head of Nefertiti,* a foreign wall calendar with a woman in a pink brassiere and a poster for a transatlantic airline. Balls of wool glowed scarlet on top of the desk...

Tanya produced a bottle of dessert wine, an apple, halva and some curled-up sweaty cheese. I asked:

"Where do you work?"

"At the Leningrad Engineering Institute, in the administration office. And you?"

"I'm a reporter," I said.

"A journalist?"

"No, a reporter. Journalism is style, ideas, problems... A reporter reports facts. A reporter's primary goal is not to lie. That is the essence of his job. For a reporter, the epitome of style is silence. It contains the fewest lies."

The conversation was becoming serious.

I generally preferred not to talk about my literary affairs. In this sense, I was keeping my so-called innocence. By gently putting down my work I was achieving the opposite effect. At least so I thought...

The wine had been drunk, the apple was cut into pieces. There was a pause, which in a situation like this could be fatal...

As strange as it may seem, I was feeling something like love.

Where did it come from? From what pile of garbage? From what depths of this wretched, miserable life? In what empty, barren soil do these exotic flowers bloom? Under the rays of which sun?

Some art studios full of junk, vulgarly dressed young ladies... Guitar, vodka, pathetic dissidence... And suddenly – dear God! – love...

How wonderfully indiscriminate He is, this king of the universe!

And then Tanya said, so quietly I could barely hear:

"Let's talk, just talk..."

A few minutes earlier I had taken off my shoes without Tanya noticing.

"In theory," I said, "it's possible. In practice – not really."

Meanwhile, I was silently cursing the broken zipper on my sweater...

A thousand times I will fall into this pit. And a thousand times I will die from fear.

The only solace is that this fear lasts less than a smoke.

Then it was cramped, and there were words that were painful to think about in the morning. But most importantly there was a morning as such, and shapes were coming into focus as they floated from out of the darkness. A morning without disappointment, which I expected and dreaded.

I remember I even said:

"And morning looks good on you..."

She was plainly more beautiful without make-up.

And that's how it all began. And lasted ten years. Just short of ten years...

I began to drop by Tanya's place from time to time. For a week I'd work from morning till night. Then, I'd visit some friend. We'd sit around, talk about Nabokov, about Joyce, about hockey and black terriers...

Sometimes I'd get drunk and then I'd call her.

"It's a mystery!" I'd yell into the receiver. "An honest-to-God mystery... I happen to call and each time you say it's already two in the morning..."

Later I would stumble to her house. It visibly jutted out against the rest, as if taking a step towards me.

Tanya continued to surprise me with her silent compliance. I didn't know what it was a reflection of – indifference, humility or pride.

She did not ask:

"When will you come over?"

Or:

"Why haven't you phoned?"

She amazed me with her unfaltering readiness for love, conversation, fun. As well as with her complete lack of any kind of initiative in this respect...

She was quiet and calm. Quiet without tension and calm without intimidation. This was the quiet calm of the ocean, indifferent to the cries of seagulls...

Like most frivolous men, I wasn't a very malicious person. I'd begin to repent or make jokes. I would say:

"Suitors can be in-patients or out-patients. I, for instance, am an out-patient..."

And then:

"What do you see in me? You should find yourself a good man! Someone in the armed services..."

"The incentive isn't there," said Tanya. "It's not exciting to love a good man..."

What interesting times we live in. "A good man" sounds like an insult to us. "But he is a good man" is said about a suitor who is clearly an insignificant nobody...

A year had passed. I dropped in on Tanya more and more frequently. Her neighbours greeted me politely and took messages for me.

I began keeping some personal belongings there. A toothbrush in a ceramic cup, an ashtray and slippers. One day I fastened a photograph of Saul Bellow over the desk.

"Belov?" asked Tanya. "From *Novy Mir*?"

"The very same," I said.

Very well, I thought, why not marry? Marry out of a sense of duty. Perhaps it'll all work out fine. And for both us.

For all intents and purposes we are married and it's going well.

A union divested of obligations. This being the guarantee of its longevity...

But what about love? What about jealousy and sleepless nights? What about the overflow of feelings? What about unsent letters with blurry ink? What about swooning at the sight of a tiny foot? What about Cupid and Amor and various other extras in this captivating show? And for that matter, what about the bouquet of flowers for a rouble thirty?

To be honest, I don't even know what love is. I am wholly without criteria. Tragic love – that I understand. But what if everything is fine? I find that disquieting. There must be a catch to this sense of normality. And yet what's even more frightening is chaos...

Let's say we make it official. But wouldn't that be amoral? Since morality will not tolerate any pressure...

Morality must flow out of our nature organically. How does it go in Shakespeare: "Thou, nature, art my goddess."*

Then again, who said it? Edmund! A rare kind of scoundrel...

So everything is getting terribly confused.

Nonetheless, a question remains: who would dare accuse a hawk or wolf of being amoral? Who would call amoral a marsh, a blizzard or the desert heat?

An imposed morality is a challenge to the forces of nature. In short, if I do marry out of a sense of duty, then it will be amoral...

Once Tanya called me herself. Of her own volition. For someone like her, that was almost subversive.

"Are you free?"

"Unfortunately not," I said. "I've got a teletype."

For about three years, I'd been turning down all unexpected invitations. The mysterious word "teletype" was supposed to sound convincing.

"My cousin is here. I've always wanted you two to meet."

And why shouldn't I meet a fellow drinker?

In the evening, I went over to Tanya's. I had a little for courage. Then a little more. At seven I rang her doorbell. And a minute later, after an awkward crush in the corridor, I saw her cousin.

He had taken a seat in the way police officers, provocateurs and midnight guests do, with his side to the table.

The lad looked strong.

A brick-brown face towered over a wall of shoulders. Its dome was crowned with a brittle and dusty patch of last year's grass. The stucco arches of his ears were swallowed up by the semi-darkness. The bastion of his wide solid forehead was missing embrasures. The gaping lips gloomed like a ravine. The flickering small swamps of his eyes, veiled by an icy cloud, questioned. The bottomless, cavernous mouth nurtured a threat.

The cousin got up and extended his left hand like a battleship. I barely suppressed a cry when his steel vice gripped my hand.

And then he collapsed onto a screeching chair. The granite millstones quivered. A short but crushing earthquake had turned the man's face into ruins for a moment. Among which bloomed, only to die shortly thereafter, a pale-red blossom of a smile.

The man introduced himself with importance:

"Erich-Maria."

"Boris." I smiled listlessly.

"And now you have met," said Tanya.

Then she went to fuss about in the kitchen.

I stayed silent, as if crushed by a heavy load. And felt his eyes on me, cold and hard, like the barrel of a rifle.

An iron hand came down on my shoulders. My flimsy jacket suddenly felt tight.

I remember I burst out with something ridiculous. Something terribly polite.

"You are forgetting yourself, maestro!"

"Silence!" uttered the man sitting opposite me, menacingly. And then:

"Why haven't you married her, you son of a bitch? What are you waiting for, scumbag?"

"If this is my conscience," a thought flashed through my mind, "then it is rather unattractive."

I began to lose my sense of reality. The contours of the world blurred hopelessly. The cousin-structure reached for the wine with interest.

I heard the tram rattle outside. I pulled at my elbows to straighten my jacket.

Then I said, as authoritatively as I could:

"Hey, cousin, please keep your hands to yourself! I've been planning to have a constructive discussion about marriage for some time. I have champagne in my briefcase. Give me a minute."

And with resolve I set the bottle on the smooth, polished table. This is how we got married.

The cousin's name was Edik Malinin, as I later found out, and he was a martial-arts instructor at a centre for deaf mutes.

But that day I evidently drank too much. Even before I showed up at Tatyana's. And must have imagined God knows what...

We got married officially in June, just before setting off for the Riga seaside. Otherwise we wouldn't have been able to stay in a hotel there.

The years passed. I couldn't get published. I was drinking more and more. And found more and more justifications for it.

For long stretches of time, we lived on Tanya's salary alone.

Our marriage combined elements of extravagance and privation. Between us, we had two separate dwellings within five tram stops of each other. Tanya had about twenty-five square metres and I – two tiny cubbyholes, six and eight metres. Putting it grandly – a bedroom and a study.

Some three years later we exchanged all that for a decent two-room apartment.

Tanya was a mysterious woman. I knew so little about her that I never ceased being amazed. Any fact about her life was to me a sensation.

Once I was astonished by an unexpectedly political outburst. Until then, I had no idea about her views. Seeing Comrade Grishin* in a newsreel, I remember my wife saying:

"He should be tried for his facial expression alone..."

So an understanding – that of partial dissidents – had been established between us.

And yet we fought often. I became more and more irritable. I was, at the same time, an unrecognized genius and a terrible hack. My desk drawers stored impressionistic novels while for money I created literary compositions about the army and navy.

I knew it displeased Tanya.

Bernovich kept insisting:

"By the time a man reaches thirty he must have resolved all his problems except literary ones…"

I couldn't do it. The amount of money I owed had long crossed that line where you stop caring. Literary officials had put my name on some sort of blacklist a while ago. I did not want to nor could I actualize myself fully in my role as a family man.

My wife brought up the subject of emigration more often. I became completely disoriented and left for Pushkin Hills.

Officially I was single, able-bodied and a standing member of the Journalists' Union. I also belonged to an appealing ethnic minority. Even Granin and Rytkheu acknowledged my literary abilities.*

Officially, I was a full-fledged creative personality.

In reality, I was on the edge of a mental breakdown.

And here she was. It was so unexpected, I found myself at a loss. She just stood there, smiling, as if everything was fine.

I heard:

"You've got some colour…"

And then, if I'm not mistaken:

"My darling…"

I asked:

"How is Masha?"

"She scratched her cheek the other day, she's so headstrong... I brought some tinned food."

"How long are you staying?"

"I have to be at work on Monday."

"You could get sick."

"Get sick with what?" Tanya was surprised.

And added:

"Actually, I'm not feeling all that well anyway."

That's some logic, I thought.

"Plus I'd feel uncomfortable," continued Tatyana. "Sima is on vacation. Roshchin is getting ready to leave for Israel. Did you know that Roshchin turned out to be Shtakelberg? And now his name isn't Dima, it's Mordechai. I'm not kidding..."

"I believe you."

"The Surises wrote; they said Leva got a good job in Boston."

"Why don't I see if I can take the day off?"

"What for? I'd like to hear the tour. I'd like to see you at work."

"This isn't real work. This is a job... I, by the way, have been writing stories for the last twenty years and you've never shown any interest..."

"You used to say fifteen. And now it's twenty. Even though it hasn't even been a year."

She had a fantastic way of making me lose my temper. But it would have been stupid to fight. People fight due to an abundance of life.

"We here are something like entertainers. We help workers have a culturally stimulating vacation."

"That's wonderful. How are your colleagues?"

"There are all kinds. We have one local guide here, Larissa, and every day she bawls over Pushkin's grave. She sees the grave and then the waterworks come…"

"Is she faking it?"

"I don't think so. A group of tourists once gave her a set of kitchen knives worth forty-six roubles."

"I wouldn't say no to that."

Just then Galina called my name. A group of tourists from Lipetsk had arrived.

I turned to Tatyana:

"You can leave your things here."

"I only have one bag."

"And you can leave it here…"

We headed towards a blue bus spattered with mud. I said hello to the driver and found a seat for my wife. Then I greeted the tourists:

"Good morning! The administration, curators and staff of Pushkin Hills welcome our guests. They have entrusted me to be your guide. My name is… This is what's to come…"

And so on.

Then I explained to the driver how to get to Mikhailovskoye. The bus started. The sounds of the radiogram drifted in as we rounded the bends:

Give the gift of fire, like Prometheus,
Give the gift of fire to big and small,
Do not begrudge the people,
The fire of your soul!

Going round the decorative boulder at a fork in the road, I said venomously:

"Pay no attention. It's just for show."

And whispered to my wife:

"These are Comrade Geychenko's dumb ideas. He wants to create an enormous amusement park here. He even hung up a chain on a tree, to make it more scenic. They say students from Tartu stole it. And dropped it in the lake. I say, bravo Structuralists!"

I led the group, stealing a glance at my wife from time to time. Her face, so attentive and a little lost, struck me anew. The pale lips, the shadow cast by her eyelashes and mournful look...

Now I was addressing her. I told her about a slight man of great genius in whom God and the Devil coexisted so easily. A man who soared high, but ended up the victim of a common earthly affliction; who created masterpieces but died the hero of a second-rate romantic novel. And who gave Bulgarin* legitimate grounds to write:

"He was a great man, who vanished like a rabbit..."

We walked along the lake. At the foot of the hill loomed another boulder. It was adorned with yet another quotation in Slavonic calligraphy. The tourists circled the rock and began snapping pictures greedily.

I lit a cigarette. Tanya came up to me.

The day was sunny, windy and not hot. A band of tourists, stretching along the shore, was catching up with us. We had to hurry.

A fat man with a notepad approached:

"Terribly sorry, what were the names of Pushkin's sons?"

"Alexander and Grigori."

"The eldest was…"

"Alexander," I said.

"And his patronymic?"

"Alexandrovich, naturally."

"And the younger?"

"What about the younger?"

"What was his patronymic?"

I looked helplessly at Tanya. My wife did not smile. She looked sad and absorbed.

"Oh, right," the tourist caught on.

We had to hurry.

"Let's go, comrades," I yelled out with pep. "Forward march to the next quotation!"

At Trigorskoye the tour went smoothly, and even felt a bit inspired. Mainly, and I repeat, due to the nature and logic of the exposition.

I was taken aback by one lady's request, though. She wanted to hear the love song 'A Magic Moment I Remember'. I told her that I couldn't sing at all. The lady insisted. The fat man with a notepad rescued me. "Why don't I sing it," he proposed…

"Please, not here," I implored. "On the bus."

(On our way back the fat man did indeed sing. Turned out this dunce was a wonderful tenor.)

I noticed that Tanya was tired, and decided to skip Trigorskoye Park. I'd done this in the past. I addressed the tourists:

"Who's been here before?"

As rule, no one has, which meant I could abridge the programme without any risk.

My tourists dashed to the bottom of the hill. Each rushing to be first on the bus even though the seats were plentiful and assigned. While we had explored Trigorskoye our drivers had used the opportunity to go for a swim. Their hair was wet.

"Let's go to the monastery," I said. "Take a left from the parking lot."

The young driver nodded and asked:

"Will you be there long?"

"No more than half an hour."

At the monastery, I introduced Tanya to the curator, Loginov. Rumour had it that Nikolai Vladimirovich was religious and even observed tradition. I wanted to talk to him about faith and waited for an opportune moment. He seemed happy and calm, and I was so lacking in that...

I concluded the tour in the southern vestry by Bruni's drawing. The ending would have been more effective by the grave, but I wanted to let the group go. My wife stood by the railing for a bit and soon returned.

"All this is sad and absurd," she said.

I didn't ask what she meant. I was tired. Or rather, I felt very tense. I knew that her visit was no accident.

"Let's have dinner at The Seashore," I offered.

"I wouldn't even mind a little to drink," replied Tanya.

The room was deserted and stuffy. Two enormous fans sat idle. The walls were adorned with wooden reliefs. The few customers comprised two groups: the visiting aristocracy, in blue jeans, and the local public, much greyer in appearance. The visitors dined. The locals drank.

We sat by the window.

"I forgot to ask how you got here? I mean I didn't have the chance."

"Very easily, on a night bus."

"You could have come with one of the guides, for free."

"I don't know them."

"Neither do I. Next time we'll arrange something in advance."

"Next time you come to us. It is rather taxing."

"Do you wish you hadn't come?"

"No, not at all! It's wonderful here..."

A waitress with a tiny notepad came to the table.

I knew this damsel. The guides nicknamed her Bismarck.

"Yeah, what?" she uttered.

And fell silent, fully debilitated.

"Is it possible to be a little more polite?" I asked. "As an exception. My wife is visiting."

"What did I say?"

"I beg you, please stop."

Then Tatyana ordered pancakes, wine, chocolates...

"Let's discuss everything. Let's speak calmly."

"I won't go. Let them leave."

"Who are 'they'?" asked Tanya.

"They are the ones who are ruining my life. Let them leave."

"They'll put you in prison."

"Let them. If literature is a pursuit deserving condemnation then our place is behind bars. And anyway, they no longer send people away for literature."

"Heifetz* hadn't even published his work and yet he got put away."

"That's precisely why they got him: because he didn't publish. He should have printed something in *Grani*. Or *Continent.** Now there's no one to fight for him. Otherwise they could have made some noise in the West."

"Are you certain?"

"Of what?"

"That Misha Heifetz is of any interest to people in the West?"

"And why not? They wrote about Bukovsky. They wrote about Kuznetsov."*

"These are all games of politics. We must think of real life."

"I'm telling you again, I will not leave."

"Can you explain why?"

"There's nothing to explain. My language, my people, my crazy country... Imagine this, I even love the policemen."

"Love is freedom. While the doors are open, everything is fine. But if the doors are locked from the outside, it becomes a prison..."

"But they're letting people out now."

"And I want to use this chance. I'm fed up. I'm fed up with standing in lines for all sorts of junk. I'm fed up with wearing stockings with holes. I'm fed up of getting excited about beef sausages... What's holding you back? The Hermitage, the Neva River, birch trees?"

"I couldn't care less about birch trees."

"Then what?"

"Language. In a foreign tongue we lose eighty per cent of our personality. We lose our ability to joke, to be ironic. This alone terrifies me."

"I don't have time for jokes. Think about Masha. Imagine what awaits her."

"You're blowing everything out of proportion. Millions of people live, work and are perfectly happy."

"Let these millions stay. I am talking about you. Either way, you are not published."

"But my readers are here. While over there... Who needs my stories in Chicago?"

"And who needs them here? The waitress at The Seashore, who hasn't even read the menu?"

"Everyone. They just don't know it yet."

"This is the way it'll always be."

"You are wrong."

"Try to understand: in ten years I'll be an old woman. And I know exactly what my life will look like. Because each day that's gone by is a step into the future, and every step is the same: grey, worn and steep... I want to live one more life. I dream of something unexpected. I don't care if it's a drama or tragedy... it'll be an unexpected drama..."

We've had this conversation time and again. I would disagree, call her to reason. Pose some kind of moral, spiritual or psychological arguments. Try to prove something.

But at the same time I knew that all my rationalizations were lies. It wasn't about that. I simply couldn't make this decision.

Such a serious and irreversible step frightened me. After all, it would be like being reborn. And at one's own will. Most people can't even get married properly...

All my life I had detested active behaviour of any kind. To my ear, the word "activist" sounds like an insult. I lived in the passive voice, so to speak, allowing circumstances to take the lead. This helped me find justification for everything.

Any decisive step imposes responsibility. So let others be held responsible. Inactivity is the only moral condition... In a perfect world, I'd become a fisherman. Sit out my life on a riverbank. And preferably without any trophies.

I didn't believe Tanya capable of leaving without me. For her, America was synonymous with divorce, I had thought. A divorce that had already formally taken place and lost its vigour, like flat beer.

In the old days women would say: "I'm going to find myself a good-looking rich guy, then you'll be sorry." Now they say: "I'm going to America."

America for me was fiction. Something like a mirage. A half-forgotten film starring Akbar the tiger and Charlie Chaplin...

"Tanya," I said, "I'm an irresponsible man and I'm up for any adventure. If the Santa María* or a Boeing was sitting out there" (I pulled back the curtain) "I'd get on and go. Just to see this Broadway. But dealing with all the red tape, explaining things, convincing them... Historical birthplace... Ancestral calling... Imaginary aunt by the name of Fanny Tsyperovich..."

Our food and drinks arrived.

"Then wish us luck... Oh look, 'potato' is spelt with two As in the menu."

"I'm sorry?"

"Anyway, I've come to say goodbye. If you don't want to go, we'll leave by ourselves. It's decided."

"And Masha?"

"What about Masha? I'm doing all this for her. Will you sign the papers?"

"What papers? Wait a minute, let's have a drink."

"That you have no material claims against us. Do you have material claims?"

"Don't be ridiculous."

"Then you'll sign the papers?"

"And what if I don't?"

"Then they won't let Masha leave."

"And you'll go alone?"

"I don't know... No... But I don't think you'll do that. Fundamentally you're not a mean person."

"What's kindness got to do with anything? We're talking about a living person. What if our daughter grows up and says... How can you decide for her?"

"And who should decide? You? You, who've ruined your life and mine..."

"All's not that hopeless."

"I urge you to think about it."

"There's nothing to think about... Some stupid papers... Why did you have to start all this? Besides, I'm not drinking. I'm working. Life will sort itself out, you'll see."

"You yourself said, 'Once a drinker, always a drinker!'"

"No, I didn't. It was some Englishman. Let him be damned!"

"It doesn't matter. Someone is trying to say hello."

I looked over. Mitrofanov and Pototsky were standing in the doorway. I was glad for the chance to stop this conversation. If I could just get her into bed, I thought...

"Let me introduce you," I said. "Sit down."

Stasik bowed ceremoniously:

"Author of novels, Pototsky. Member of the SU of Writers."

Mitrofanov nodded without saying anything.

"Join us. Do you have time?"

"I've done time," Pototsky replied playfully.

Mitrofanov maintained silence.

I realized they had no money and said:

"My wife is visiting. It's on me."

And I went up to the bar to get us some beers. When I returned, Pototsky was saying something animatedly to my wife. I could tell he was talking about his talent and the outrageousness of censorship. Which, however, did not hamper his departure from the subject:

"Beer? I'm afraid it won't irrigate the system..."

I had no choice but to get vodka. By that time the waitress had brought our sandwiches and salad.

Pototsky became visibly invigorated.

"For me – a large one," he said. "I love the larger ones."

Volodya still hadn't said anything. Stasik noticed my look of curiosity and explained, pointing to Mitrofanov:

"You see, a wasp flew into his mouth."

"Dear God," sighed my wife. "Is it still in there?"

"Not any more. He was finishing a tour of the monastery, you see, and a wasp flew into his mouth. Volodya, beg your pardon, hawked up, but it whooped him all the same. Now he can't speak – it hurts."

"And does it hurt to swallow?" asked Tanya.

Volodya shook his head vigorously.

"Swallowing doesn't hurt," clarified Pototsky.

I poured them vodka. It was evident that this company was burdensome for my wife.

"How do you like it here?" asked Pototsky.

"Some parts are wonderful. Like the view of Savkin Hill, or Kern Lane…"

Suddenly Mitrofanov tensed up.

"Fa-fa-fee," he uttered.

"What?" asked my wife.

"Fa-fa-fee," repeated Mitrofanov.

"He says it's all 'fantasy'," explained Pototsky. "He wants to say that Kern Lane is nothing more than director Geychenko's invention. I mean, the lane exists, of course – your typical lane with linden trees. But Anna Kern had nothing to do with it. It's possible she's never been anywhere near this lane."

"But I like to think that it was just there that Pushkin told this woman how he felt."

"She was a courtesan," Pototsky insisted sternly.

"Mo-mo-ho," added Mitrofanov.

"Volodya wants to say 'common whore'. And, forgive me for being rude, he is right. Anna Petrovna had dozens of lovers.

Comrade Glinka alone is worth volumes... And what about Nikitenko? And to get mixed up with a censor – that's crossing all boundaries!"

"Back then censorship was different," said my wife.

"Any censorship is a crime." Stasik did not miss an opportunity to jump on a topic close to his heart.

"My entire life is a fight against censorship," he went on. "Any censorship abuses the artist... Censorship sparks an alcoholic protest in me! Let's drink to the end of censorship!"

Stasik had another drink and mysteriously lowered his voice:

"*Antra noo!* Between us! For a while now I've been hatching a plan to emigrate. I have in me exactly one thirty-second part of Jewish blood. And I have my eye set on the post of President's advisor. I am the keeper of a secret recipe for making Tula honey cakes."

"Oh-eh," said Mitrofanov.

"What do you mean 'loaded'?" objected Pototsky. "Yes, I had something to drink. Yes, I am slightly uninhibited. And yes, I am stirred by the company of a beautiful lady. But ideologically I am sober."

There was a painful silence. Then someone dropped a coin into an apparatus called "Meloman" and the heart-rending wailing of Anatoly Korolyov* broke through:

"The city held to me

Its open hand of squares,

The leaves along the boulevard are turning gold...

There is so much I need to say to you,

But who will help me find the perfect words?"

"We have to go," I said. "Should I order more vodka?"

Stasik cast down his eyes. Mitrofanov nodded enthusiastically.

I ordered and paid. We rose to leave.

Pototsky jumped up and clicked his worn-down heels:

"As my noble Polish ancestors used to say – *do widzenia!*"*

Mitrofanov smiled sadly.

The short walk led through the woods. Damp and cold crept from behind the trees. Endless cyclists were passing us by. The path was intersected with pine roots and the wheel rims jangled sharply.

Tanya was saying:

"Perhaps my decision is adventurism or even madness. But I've had enough..."

Her desperation frightened me. But what could I say?

"Do you remember the time when I carried you home? I held you in my arms and then I dropped you... There was a time when everything was good. And it will be again."

"We were such different people then. I am getting older."

"Nothing of the kind..."

Tanya fell silent. I, as usual, launched into discourse:

"The only honest path is the path of mistakes, disappointments and hopes. Life is the discovery of the boundaries of good and evil through personal experience. There is no other way. I have arrived somewhere... I think it's not too late..."

"These are words."

"But words are my profession."

"And these, too, are words. It's all been decided. Come with us. You'll live another life..."

"For a writer it equals death."

"There are a lot of Russians there."

"They are defeatists. A bunch of miserable defeatists. Even Nabokov is a flawed talent. So what's there to say about some Zurov!"

"Who is this Zurov?"

"There was a guy..."

"What are we talking about? It's done. I'm going to file all the papers on Thursday."

Absent-mindedly I counted the days till Thursday.

And suddenly I felt such acute pain, such inexplicable bitterness, that I even choked up. I said:

"Tanya, forgive me and don't leave."

"It's too late," she said, "darling."

I walked ahead of her and started to cry. Or rather, I didn't cry, I stopped holding myself back. As I walked, I kept repeating: "Dear God! What am I being punished for?" And I replied to myself in my head: "What do you mean, what for? For everything. For your sordid, lazy and reckless life..."

Behind me walked my wife – distant, resolute and courageous. And not quite as foolish, as it turned out...

We reached the top of the hill. I pointed out the house in which I lived. A thin line of smoke rose vertically from the chimney. That meant the landlord was home.

We walked through a village street and all the people greeted us with a smile. I noticed long ago that people liked us as a couple. When I'm alone, things are different.

Suddenly Nadezhda Fyodorovna said:

"Come by for milk in the morning."

The roosters and the shaggy pups amused Tanya, but when she saw a turkey there was no limit to her delight:

"What aplomb! What pomposity! All given his rather heinous appearance. The roosters and geese are also putting on airs, but this guy... My God, he looks just like Isaacson!"

Seeing us, Mikhail Ivanych became terribly animated. With a doleful grimace he did up the shirt buttons on his permanently brown neck. So much so that the wrinkled corners of his collar turned up. And he put on a peaked cap for some reason.

"Borya and I are doing good," he said, "in terms of behaviour and in general... In the sense – no white, no red, no beer... Not to mention cologne... He just reads those books. He reads and he reads and he'll die a fool," concluded Mikhail Ivanych unexpectedly.

I tried to neutralize him somehow and called him to the hallway:

"Misha, do you need money?"

"Whatsa? Eh... OK..."

I shoved three notes in his hand.

"The Cavalier is open till eleven," said Mikhail Ivanych. "I'll make it. Or take Alexei's mare... And where were you earlier, eh? They had apple wine for a roub fourteen at the settlement. So, I'm off. There's salt pork and onions over there..." he hollered from the threshold.

It was just the two of us now. Tanya looked around the place with fear.

"Are you sure this room is inhabitable?"

"There was a time when I had my doubts. I've straightened the place up. You should've seen it before."

"There are holes in the roof."

"You hardly notice it in good weather. And there's no rain forecast, I think."

"There are gaps between the floorboards."

"This is nothing. In the beginning stray dogs would use them to visit me."

"The gaps are still there."

"But I domesticated the dogs."

Tanya touched the blanket.

"Christ, is this what you use as a cover?"

"It's warm now," I said. "There's no need to cover oneself. Least of all you."

"Was that a compliment?"

"Something like that."

"You've lost weight."

"I walk a lot."

"It suits you."

"I also have rather large eyes…"

"This is a totally ridiculous conversation," said Tanya.

"Well, wonderful. I'd like to attain complete idiocy, buy an aquarium with little fish and a palm tree in a wooden bucket…"

"Why do you need an aquarium?"

"Why do I need a palm tree?"

"Let's start with the aquarium."

"All my life, I've dreamt of having a couple of trained goldfish."

"And the palm tree?"

"You could sketch a palm tree from nature. And keep it on the balcony."

"In what life do we have a balcony, I'd like to know?"

"It's not like we already have the palm tree..."

"Dear Lord, what am I asking? And what are we talking about?"

"Really, what should we talk about? Especially when all's been decided."

I looked at the windows. There were no curtains. Anyone could have looked in. In village life, things were basic.

I could move the wardrobe, I thought. I looked around and didn't see one...

"What's new in Leningrad?" I asked.

"I told you. Some people are getting ready to leave, others despise them for it."

"Did Mitya call?"

"He calls occasionally. Things have got very bad between him and Galina. There's a Yugoslav in the picture... Or a Hungarian, I can't remember... His name is Achil—"

"An ancient Greek perhaps?"

"No, I remember that he's from the socialist camp... Anyway, Mitya is beside himself. He became really angry, sort of like you. He wanted to beat up Zhenya Kreyn..."

"And Zhenya?"

"Zhenya said to him: 'Mitya, I'm not afraid of you because you have horns. Thus it follows that you are not predatory...' They barely managed to pull them apart."

"That's a shame..."

There was a silence.

I was still trying to find something to put on the windows. And do it in a way that seemed spontaneous and effortless.

We've been married ten years and yet I still die with fear. Afraid that Tanya will pull her hand away and say: "That's all I need!"

And yet I've managed to take off my shoes. I always take my shoes off ahead of time so as not to get distracted later... So as not to have to say: "Just a minute, I need to take off my shoes..." Plus the laces get tangled in the nervous haste. I must have torn a thousand of them in the throes of passion.

"I also met Guryev, a known dissident. You must have heard of him, he's been mentioned on Western radio stations. Frieda introduced us. We were at his house, on Pushkin Street, talking about emigration. His home is full of icons..."

"Then he must be a Jew."

"So it seems. But his last name is Russian – Guryev."

"That's what's suspicious. Guryev... Guryevich..."

"What do you have against Jews?"

"Nothing. Especially since this one is Russian. I've known him since '65."

"So you're kidding me again."

"That's because I'm a kidder."

"Guryev is really smart. He says that Russia is experiencing a Christian renaissance. That it's an irreversible process. And that in the cities, sixty per cent of the population is religious, while it's seventy-five in the country."

"Mikhail Ivanych being one, for example."

"I don't know Mikhail Ivanych. He makes a good impression."

"Yeah, not bad. Only his saintliness is a bit lacking..."

"Guryev treated us to instant coffee. He said: 'You're using too much... I'm not being frugal, it's just that it changes the flavour...' And when we were getting ready to leave, he said, 'I'll walk you to the bus. There's some mischief in these parts. Hoodlums everywhere...' And Frieda says to him, 'Don't worry, only forty per cent...' Guryev got touchy and changed his mind about walking us there. What are you doing? At least turn off the light!"

"Why?"

"That's what people do."

"I can drape my jacket over the window and put my hat on the lamp. We'll have a night light."

"It's not very sanitary."

"You'd think you were from Andalusia!"

"Don't look."

"As if I come across beauty a lot."

"My pantyhose are full of holes."

"Banish them from my sight!"

"There you go again." Tanya's feelings were hurt. "And I came here for a serious talk."

"Just put it out of your mind," I said, "at least for half an hour."

I heard footsteps from the vestibule. Misha had come back. Muttering, he got into bed.

I was worried that he'd start swearing. My fears were confirmed.

"Maybe we could turn on the radio?" asked Tanya.

"There is no radio. But there is an electric grinder…"

It took Misha a long time to settle down. A philosophical note was discernible in his profanities. For example, I heard:

"Eh, swimming upstraddle, up yours, with no paddle…"

Finally it was quiet. We were together again. Tanya suddenly got loud. I said:

"Keep it down. Let's not wake Misha."

"What can I do?"

"Try thinking about something else. I always think about my problems. Like my debts, aches and pains, the fact that I can't get published."

"And I think about you. You are my biggest problem."

"Do you want some country salt pork?"

"No. Do you know what I want?"

"I can guess…"

Tanya was crying again. She was saying such things that all I could think of was whether Misha would wake up. Wouldn't he be surprised…

And then I smelt fumes. My imported cap was shrouded in a cloud of smoke. I turned off the lamp but it was already light. The oilcloth gleamed.

"The first bus leaves at nine thirty," my wife said. "The next one is at four. I still need to pick up Masha…"

"I'll get you on a bus for free. There's a Petersburg three-day tour that leaves at ten."

"I won't be imposing?"

"Not at all. They have a huge 'Icarus' luxury bus. There's always a free seat."

"Maybe I should give something to the driver?"

"That's my problem. We keep our own tally... OK, I'm off to get milk."

"Put your pants on."

"That's an idea..."

Nadezhda Fyodorovna was already pottering around in the garden. Her blooming behind rose over the potato vines. She asked:

"So that was your gal?"

"My wife," I said.

"It's hard to believe. She looks too nice."

The woman looked me over scornfully.

"Guys got it good. The worse they are, the prettier the wives."

"What's so bad about me?"

"You look like Stalin."

Stalin was not loved in the countryside. I noticed this a while ago. Evidently, they still remembered collectivization and his other tricks. Our creative intelligentsia could learn a thing or two from the illiterate peasants. They say the entire auditorium of the Leningrad Palace of Arts burst into applause when Stalin appeared on screen.

But I have always hated him. Long before Khrushchev's reforms. Long before I learnt how to read. Political credit for this belongs to my mother. My mother, an Armenian from Tbilisi, criticized Stalin unrelentingly, albeit in a rather idiosyncratic manner. She repeated with conviction:

"A Georgian cannot be a decent man!"

I walked back, trying not to spill the milk. Tanya was up. She washed her face and made the bed. Mikhail Ivanych was fixing his power saw and grunting. There was a smell of smoke, grass and sun-baked clover in the air.

I poured the milk, sliced the bread, and got out some green onions and hard-boiled eggs. Tanya was examining my ruined hat.

"I can put a leather patch on it if you like?"

"What for? It's warm already."

"I'll send you a new one."

"I have a better idea, maybe some cyanide."

"No, I'm serious, what should I send you?"

"How should I know what they've got in America these days? Let's not talk about it."

We reached the tourist centre a little before nine. The driver had already turned the bus around. The tourists were stacking their bags and suitcases in the luggage compartment. Some had taken their seats by the windows. I walked up to the driver I knew:

"Got any free seats?"

"For you, not a problem."

"I want to send my wife to Leningrad."

"I sympathize. I'd like to send mine to Kamchatka. Or to the moon, instead of Gagarin."

The driver was wearing an attractive imported shirt. As a rule, drivers of tour buses were fairly cultured. Most of them could easily have replaced the guides. Only they'd be taking a significant pay cut…

From the corner of my eye, I saw that Tanya was talking to

Marianna Petrovna. For some reason I always feel alarmed when two women are left alone. Especially when one of them is my wife.

"OK, then it's settled," I said to the driver. "Drop her off on Obvodny Canal."

"It's too shallow," the driver laughed.

I should just get on the bus, I thought, and leave as well. One of the guides can bring my things. Only what will we live on? And how?

Galina dashed past us, nodding in the direction of my wife: "My goodness, how plain!"

I didn't say anything. But in my mind I set her peroxide-bleached locks on fire.

The sports instructor, Seryozha Yefimov, approached.

"My excuses," he said. "This is for you." And he put a jar of blackberries in Tanya's hands.

We had to say goodbye.

"Call me," Tanya said.

I nodded.

"Is there a phone you can use?"

"Of course. Give Masha a kiss. How long will all this take?"

"It's hard to tell. A month, maybe two... Think about it."

"I'll call."

The driver climbed behind the wheel. The imported motor roared with confidence. I blurted out something unintelligible.

"And I..." said Tanya.

The bus started and quickly turned the corner. A minute later, its crimson side flashed through the trees near Lugovka.

I popped into the office. My group from Kiev was arriving at noon. I had to go back home.

On the table, I saw Tanya's hairpins, two dirty cups from the milk, leftover bread and eggshells. There was a barely perceptible scent of smoke and cosmetics.

When she left, Tanya said, "And I..." The rest was drowned out by the drone of the motor...

I looked in on Mikhail Ivanych. He wasn't there. A shotgun glimmered above his dirty bed. A Tula-made, heavy double-barrelled gun with a reddish stock. I took down the gun and thought – isn't it time for me to shoot myself?

June turned out dry and clear, with grass rustling underfoot. Multicoloured towels hung off the tourist-centre balconies. The sturdy snap of tennis balls resounded. Bicycles with shiny rims glowed ruby along the wide porch railing. The sounds of an old tango carried through from the speaker above the attic window. The melody seemed traced over a dashed line...

The snap of the balls, the smell of scorched earth and the geometry of the bicycles were the things I'll remember about this unhappy June...

I called Tanya twice. And each time it felt awkward. It felt like her life was following a rhythm different from my own. I felt silly, like a fan who'd jumped out onto a football field.

There were strange voices in our apartment. Tanya would ask me unexpected questions. For instance:

"Where do we keep electricity bills?"

Or:

"Would you mind if I sold my gold chain?"

I didn't even know that my wife owned anything valuable…

Tanya ran from pillar to post filing documents. She complained about bureaucrats and bribe-takers.

"I have in my bag," she said, "ten bars of chocolate, four tickets to see Kobzon and three copies of Tsvetaeva's poetry…"*

Tanya seemed excited and almost happy.

What could I say to her? Beg her for the tenth time, "Do not leave?"

I felt humiliated by her absorption in her own affairs. What about me with my problems of an almost dissident?

Tanya had no time for me. Finally something important was happening…

Once she called me herself. Luckily I was at the tourist centre. At the library in the main building, actually. I had to run across the entire facility. It turned out Tanya needed a document giving her permission to take the child. Saying I had no material claims.

Tanya dictated a few official phrases. I remember these words: "…a child in the amount of one…"

"Have it notarized there and send it to me. That will be simplest."

"I can come to you," I said.

"Right now that's not necessary."

There was a pause.

"But will we have time to say goodbye?"

"Of course. Please don't think…"

She was almost making excuses. She felt guilty because of her disregard. For her hasty "that's not necessary"…

Evidently, I'd become an agonizing problem that she had managed to solve. In other words, someone from her past. With all my vices and virtues. None of which mattered any more...

That day I got drunk. Got myself a bottle of vodka and finished it all on my own.

I didn't want to invite Misha – conversations with him required too much effort. They reminded me of my university chats with Professor Likhachyov. Only with Likhachyov I made the effort to appear smarter and with this one, just the opposite – I tried to be as plain and simple as I could.

For example, Mikhail Ivanych would ask:

"You know why Jews have their knobs snipped? So their joysticks work better..."

And I agreed, amiably:

"I guess so... I suppose that's what it is..."

Anyway, I walked to the grove near the bathhouse and sat resting against a birch tree. I drank a bottle of Moskovskaya vodka on an empty stomach, chain-smoking and chewing on rowanberries.

The world didn't improve right away. At first I was disturbed by the mosquitoes. Some slimy thing kept trying to crawl up my leg. And the grass felt soggy.

Eventually, everything changed. The woods parted, encircled me and welcomed me into their sultry bosom. For a time, I felt myself a harmonious part of the universal whole. The bitterness of the rowanberry seemed inseparable from the damp smell of the grass. The leaves overhead vibrated slightly from the buzzing of mosquitoes. The clouds floated by, as if on a TV screen, and even a spider's web looked like a jewel.

I felt ready to cry, though I still understood it was the alcohol's doing. Evidently, harmony hides itself at the bottom of the bottle...

I kept saying to myself:

"Pushkin too had debts and an uneasy relationship with the government. Plus the trouble with his wife, not to mention his difficult temperament...

"And so what? They opened a museum. Hired tour guides – forty of them. And each one loves Pushkin madly...

"Where were you all before, I'd like to know? And who is the butt of your collective derision now?"

I never got an answer to my questions. I fell asleep...

When I woke up it was almost eight. Twigs and branches beamed black against the pale, ash-grey clouds. The insects came to life... The spider's web touched my face...

I got up, feeling the heaviness of my sticky clothes.

My matches were damp. As was my money. But more importantly, there was very little of it left: six roubles. The thought of vodka loomed like a dark cloud...

I didn't want to go through the tourist centre. At this hour it was full of idling methodologists and tour guides. Any one of them might have started a serious conversation about the director of the Lyceum, Yegor Antonovich Englehardt.

I had to walk around the tourist centre and make my way to the road through the woods.

Cutting through the courtyard of the monastery also frightened me. The very atmosphere of a monastery is unbearable for a man with a hangover.

And so I continued downhill along the route through the woods. More of a broken footpath, actually.

It began to ease off a bit by the time I reached the Cavalier. Compared to local drunks, I looked like a prig.

The door was held open with a rubber brick. On display in the hallway by the mirror was a ridiculous wooden sculpture – a creation of the retired Major Goldstein. The copper sign read: "Goldstein, Abraham Saulovich". And below it, in quotes: "The Russian".

"The Russian" brought to mind both Mephistopheles and Baba Yaga.* The wooden helmet was painted silver with gouache.

Eight people or so were crowding around the snack bar. Wrinkled roubles soundlessly landed on the counter. Coins jangled in the chipped saucer.

Two or three groups were partying by the wall in the main room. They talked energetically with their hands, coughed and laughed. These were workers from the tourist centre, psychiatric-hospital orderlies and stable hands from the lumber mill.

The local intelligentsia – a film projectionist, an art restorer and entertainment organizer – kept apart, at different tables. Facing the wall was a man I did not recognize, wearing a green polo shirt and domestically manufactured jeans. His ginger locks rested on his shoulders.

It was my turn at the bar. I felt the familiar hangover shakes. Under the soggy jacket throbbed my weary, orphaned soul.

I had to maximize my six roubles. They had to stretch as far as they would go.

I ordered a bottle of fortified wine and two chocolates. I could get two more rounds like this and there would still be twenty copecks left over for cigarettes.

I sat by the window. Now there was no rush.

Outside two gypsies were unloading crates of bread from a car. A postman surged up the hill on his moped. Stray dogs were rolling around in the dirt.

I got down to business. And made a positive mental note: my hands aren't shaking. Which was good...

The wine was spreading like good news, colouring the world with hues of kindness and compassion.

Ahead of me lay divorce, debt and literary failure... But here are these mysterious gypsies with bread... Two dark-skinned old women near the polyclinic... A damp day cooling off... Wine, a free minute, my homeland...

Through the general din I suddenly heard:

"This is Moscow! This is Moscow! You are listening to the Young Pioneers' Dawn... At the microphone is the hirsute Yevstikheyev... His words sound like a commendable rebuff to the vultures from the Pentagon..."

I looked around. This mysterious speech was coming from the fellow in the green polo shirt. He was still facing the wall. Even from behind you could see how drunk he was. His back, covered with rippling locks, expressed some sort of aggressive impatience. He was almost yelling:

"And I say no! No to the overreaching imperialist beasts! No, echo the workers of the Ural paper mill... There is no happiness in life, my dear listeners! I say this to you as the last man standing of the 316th Rifle Division... Thus spoke Zarathustra..."

People in the restaurant began to listen. Although without real interest.

The guy raised his voice:

"What are you staring at, you schlubs? You want to behold the death of a private in the Guards of the Maykop Artillery Regiment, Viscount de Bragelonne?* Allow me to grant you that chance... Comrade Rappoport, bring in the prisoner!"

The other patrons reacted peaceably. Though "schlubs" was clearly meant for them.

Someone from the corner said indifferently:

"Valera's a bit pickled..."

Valera rose energetically:

"The right to rest and recreation is guaranteed by the constitution... As in the finest houses of Paris and Brussels... Then why turn the sciences into a slave of theology? Live up to the agenda of the Twentieth Assembly of the Party! Listen to the Young Pioneers' Dawn... Text brought to you by Gmyrya..."

"Who?" someone asked from the corner.

"Baron Kleinmichel, lovey!"

Even at just a quick glance at the fellow I felt a sense of alarm. On closer inspection, this feeling intensified.

Long-haired, ridiculous and scraggy, he gave the impression of someone feigning schizophrenia. But with the single-minded determination of being exposed as soon as possible.

He could have passed for a lunatic were it not for his

triumphant smile and expression of common everyday tom-foolery. A cunning, shrewd insolence was detectable in his crazy monologues. In this stomach-churning mixture of newspaper headlines, slogans and unfamiliar quotations...

It all reminded me of a faulty loudspeaker. The man expressed himself sharply, spasmodically, with afflictive grandiloquence and a sort of dramatic vigour.

He was drunk, but even in that one felt some cunning.

I did not notice him come up. Only just now he sat there facing the wall. And suddenly he was looking over my shoulder:

"Let's get acquainted – Valery Markov! Habitual transgressor of the public peace..."

"Ah, yes," I said. "I heard."

"I've been a guest at the big house. The diagnosis is chronic alcoholism!"

I tilted the bottle in friendship. A glass materialized miraculously in his hand.

"Much obliged," he said. "I trust all this was bought at the price of moral degradation?"

"Quit it," I said. "Let's drink instead."

In response I heard:

"I thank you and I accede, like Shepilov..."*

We finished the wine.

"Honey on the wounds," asserted Markov.

"I have," I said, "about four roubles. Beyond that, the outlook is foggy..."

"Money is not a problem!" exclaimed my drinking companion.

He jumped up and darted to his abandoned table. When he returned he was holding a crumpled black envelope for photo paper. A pile of money spilt onto the table. He winked and said:

"You can't count diamonds in caves of stone!"

And further, with an unexpected shyness in his voice:

"It doesn't look good with the pockets bulging..."

Markov patted his hips, in skin-tight jeans. His feet were shod in patent-leather concert slippers.

What a character, I thought.

Next thing I knew, he started sharing his problems with me:

"I make a lot... The minute I'm off a bender, I'm rolling in dough... One snapshot – and I got a rouble... One morning – and there's three tenners in my pocket... By nightfall I've made a hundred... And zero financial control... What am I to do?... Drink... We've got ourselves the Kursk Magnetic Anomaly* here. A day of work followed by a week of drink... For some, vodka is a celebration. For me, it's hard reality. It's either the drunk tank or the militia – it's pure dissidence... Needless to say, the wife's not happy. We need a cow, she says... Or a child... Provided you don't drink. But for now I'm abstaining. In the sense that I still drink..."

Markov stuffed the money back in the envelope. Two or three notes fell on the floor. He was too lazy to bend down. His aristocratic behaviour reminded me of Mikhail Ivanych.

We walked up to the bar and ordered a bottle of Agdam. I reached out to pay. My companion raised his voice:

"Hands off socialist Cuba!"

And proudly threw three roubles on the bar.

A Russian drunk is a fascinating creature. Even when he has money, he still prefers poison at a rouble forty. And he won't take the change. I myself am the same...

We returned to the window. The restaurant had filled up. Someone even started to play the accordion.

"I recognize you, Mother Russia!" exclaimed Markov, and added, lowering his voice: "I hate it... I hate these Pskov buffoons! Beg your pardon, let's have a drink first."

We had a drink. It was becoming noisier. The accordion was piercing the air.

My new acquaintance was yelling excitedly:

"Just look at this progressive humanity! At these dumb faces! At these shadows of forgotten ancestors!... I live here like a ray of light in the kingdom of darkness... If only the American militarists would enslave us! Maybe then we'd live like people, of the Czech variety..."

He slammed his hand on the table:

"I want freedom! I want abstractionism with dodecacophony!... Let me tell you..."

He leant over and whispered hoarsely into my ear:

"I'll tell you like a friend... I had an idea – to get the hell out of here, and go anywhere. Even to Southern Rhodesia. As far away from our backwater as possible... But how? Our borders are bolted! From morning till night they're under the watchful eye of Karatsupa...* Go overseas as a sailor – but the local council won't let me... Marry some foreign tourist? Some ancient Greek slut? And where am I going to find her? This one character said they were letting out the Jews. And I said to my wife: 'Vera, it's our Cape of Good Hope...'

"My wife is from the simple folk. She scoffed at me. 'Your mug alone demands punitive action... They barely let your type into the movies and you want to go to Israel!'

"But I had a chat with this guy. He suggested I marry a Jew for a short while. That's much simpler. Foreign tourists are few and far between, but Jews – they do come across once in a while. There's one at the tourist centre. Named Natella. She looks Jewish, only she's fond of a tipple..."

Markov lit up a cigarette, first ruining a few matches. I began to feel drunk. Agdam was spreading through my blood vessels. The shouts were merging into a measured, swelling din.

My drinking companion was no drunker than before. And his madness seemed to have abated a little.

Twice we went to the bar for more wine. Once some people took our seats. But Markov made a scene and they left.

He shouted at their backs:

"Hands off Vietnam and Cambodia! The border is locked! Karatsupa never sleeps! Persons of Jewish nationality excepted!"

Our table was covered in candy wrappers. We flicked our ashes into a dirty saucer.

Markov continued:

"I used to think I'd make for Turkey in a kayak. And I even bought a map. But they'll sink me, the scum... So that's over. My past and thoughts, as they say... Now I'm counting more on the Jews... One time Natella and I were drinking by the river. And I said to her, 'Let's get married, the two of us.' And she said, 'You're so savage, so scary. The black earth is raging inside you,' she said... In these parts, by the way, no one's heard of black earth. But I didn't say anything. Even squeezed her a bit. And she started screaming, 'Let go of me!' I guess... So I said, 'This is how our Slavic ancestors lived...' Anyway, it didn't work... Maybe I should have asked her nicely? Should have said, 'You're a person of Jewish nationality. Help out a Russian dissident, regarding Israel...'"

Once again Markov took out his black envelope. I never got the chance to spend my four roubles...

Now we were talking, interrupting one another. I told him about my troubles. To my chagrin, I discoursed on literature.

Markov addressed the void:

"Off with your hats, gentlemen! Before you sits a genius!"

The fans chased clouds of tobacco smoke around the room. The sounds of the jukebox were drowned out by the drunken voices. Workers of the state lumber mill made a bonfire on a porcelain platter. Dogs wandered under the tables...

Everything was beginning to blur before my eyes. I managed to catch only some random bits of what Markov was saying:

"Forward to the West! Tanks moving in a diamond formation! A journey of a thousand miles begins with a single step!"

Then some intoxicated character with an accordion approached me. Its bellows blushed pink, intimately. Tears streamed down the accordion player's cheeks. He asked:

"Why'd they dock me six roubles? Why'd they take away my sick days?"

"Take a swig, Tarasych." Markov pushed the bottle towards him. "Drink and don't be upset. Six roubles is nothing..."

"Nothing?" suddenly the accordion player got angry. "People break their backs and for him it's nothing! For six years these hands drudged away for nothing doing hard time... Article 92, without an instrument..."*

In response, Markov trilled soulfully:

"Stop shedding tears, girl! The rains will pass..."

A second later, two lumber-mill stable hands were prying them apart. With a painful howl the accordion collided with the floor.

I wanted to stand up, but couldn't.

Then a Duralumin stool flew out from under me. As I fell, I took down a heavy brown curtain.

I couldn't manage to get up, even though I think Markov was taking a beating. I heard his tragic cries:

"Let me go, you beasts! *Finita la commedia!*"*

It's not that I was thrown out of the restaurant. I crawled out on my own, sheathed in the drapery fabric. Then I hit my head on the doorpost and everything went black...

I came to in a strange room. It was already light. The clock was ticking; it had a chisel for a weight.

I was still covered by the same brown drape. On the floor nearby I discovered Markov. Evidently, he had given me his bed.

My head hurt. I felt a deep gash on my forehead.

The sour odour of a peasant home made me a little sick.

I groaned. Markov raised himself up.

"Are you alive?" he asked.

"I think so. What about you?"

"Status: heading into the storm! How much do you weigh?"

"No idea, why?"

"I barely managed to drag you here…"

The door opened and a woman with a clay pot entered.

"Vera," shouted Markov. "Hair of the dog! I know you've got some. Who needs this road to Calvary? Bring it to us now! Let's bypass this interim period of developed socialism…"

"Drink some milk," said Vera.

I said hello with dignity. Markov sighed:

"And I had to be born in these boreal backwoods…"

Vera was a pale, tired woman with large, calloused hands. Cantankerous, like all wives of alcoholics, without exception.

A look of deep and utmost sorrow was etched on her face.

I also felt awkward because I was occupying the master bed. What's more, my slacks were missing. But the jacket was on.

"I'm sorry to have put you out," I said.

"Don't worry," said Vera. "We're used to it."

This was a typical village abode. The walls were flecked with reproductions from *Ogonyok* magazine.* A TV with a blurry magnifying lens hid in the corner. A faded bluish oilcloth covered the table. A portrait of Julius Fučík* hung above my headboard. A cat sauntered between the chairs. It moved soundlessly, like in an animated film.

"Where are my trousers?" I asked.

"Vera undressed you," replied Markov. "Ask her."

"I took off the trousers," explained Vera, "but I felt awkward about the jacket."

I felt too weak to process the meaning.

"That's logical," quipped Markov.

"They're in the hall, I'll get them."

"Better get us a drink first!"

Markov raised his voice a little. Arrogance and self-abasement constantly alternated in him. He said:

"A Russian dissident has got to have hair of the dog, don't you think? What would the academic Sakharov say?"*

And the next minute:

"Vera, give me some cologne! Give me some cologne with the seal of quality."

Vera brought me my trousers. I got dressed. Then put on my shoes, after shaking the pine needles out. With disgust I lit up a cigarette...

The heavy taste of morning blocked out the shame of yesterday.

Markov felt great. His groaning, I thought, was only for show.

I asked:

"Where's the envelope of money?"

"Shhh... In the attic," said Markov, and added at full volume: "Let's go! We should not await favours from nature. To take them – that is our task."

I said:

"Vera, I'm sorry for the way things happened. I hope we meet again... under different circumstances..."

"Where you going?" asked Vera. "Again? Do keep an eye on my fool."

I gave her a crooked smile, so as to say that I myself don't set a very good example...

That day we paid a call on four drinking joints. With apologies, we returned the brown curtain. We drank at the boathouse, at the film projectionist's booth and by the monastery fence.

Markov drained his sixth bottle and said:

"Some are of the opinion that a modest obelisk should be erected here!"

And he stood the bottle on the knoll.

We lost the envelope of money several times. We hugged it out with last night's accordion player. Were seen by every senior worker at the tourist centre. And according to Natella, claimed to be Pushkin and Baratynsky.*

Even Mikhail Ivanych preferred to keep away from us. Though we invited him. He did say:

"I know Valera. You knock back a few with him and find yourself sobering up at the precinct."

Thankfully, Mitrofanov and Pototsky were away on an excursion in Boldino.

We fell asleep in someone's hayloft in Petrovskoye. In the morning, this nightmare started over. Even the stable hands from the lumber mill recoiled from us.

What's more, Markov was going around with a lilac lampshade on his head. I was missing a left sleeve.

Loginov came up to us by the shop and asked:

"How is it that you're without a sleeve?"

"I was getting hot," I said, "and threw it away."

The keeper of the monastery mused over this and then made the sign of the cross over us both. Markov said:

"You shouldn't have... Instead of God, we now have Lenin's Central Committee. But there'll come a time when these bitches have their own great terror..."

Loginov looked uncomfortable, crossed himself and rushed away.

And we continued to stagger around the Preserve.

I made it home towards the end of the week. And spent the next twenty-four hours in bed, without moving. Mikhail Ivanych offered me wine. I turned to face the wall without saying anything.

Then a girl from the tourist centre named Lyuda showed up.

"You have a telegram," she said. "And Major Belyaev is looking for you."

"Belyaev who? From where?"

"Our old man says from the Ministry of the Interior."

"Just what I need! Can you tell him I'm unwell? That I'm unwell and in Pskov…"

"He knows."

"What does he know?"

"That you've been unwell for quite a few days. He said, 'Tell him to stop by after he sleeps it off.'"

"Stop by where?"

"The building next to the post office. Anyone will show you. Here's the telegram."

Shyly, the girl faced the other way and removed from her bra a bluish scrap of paper folded to the size of a postage stamp.

I unfolded the warm telegram and read:

"Flying Wed. night. Tanya. Masha."

Only five words and some cryptic numbers.

"What day is it today?"

"It was Tuesday this morning," joked Lyuda.

"When did you receive the telegram?"

"Marianna brought it from Voronich."

"When?"

"I told you, Saturday."

I wanted to say, "And where were you before?" but changed my mind. They were where they were supposed to be. A better question was: where was I?

The earliest I could leave was on the evening bus. I'd get into Leningrad around six in the morning...

"He knows all about the telegram," Lyuda said.

"Who?"

"Comrade Belyaev."

Lyuda was a tiny bit proud of the acuity and omniscience of this foreboding major.

"Comrade Belyaev said that you should see him before you leave. Or you'll get an ass-kicking... His exact words..."

"What old-fashioned courtesy!" I said...

Feverishly, I tried to collect my thoughts. My money added up to around four roubles. Still the same mystical four roubles. I felt horrible...

"Lyuda," I asked, "do you have any money?"

"Around forty copecks... I took the bike..."

"And?"

"Take my bicycle, I'll walk. Leave it with someone in the settlement..."

The last time I rode a bike I was a schoolboy. Back then it seemed like a fun thing to do. Evidently I had aged.

The road was gnarled with pine roots. The bicycle clanked as it bobbed up and down. The small hard saddle traumatized my behind. The wheels kept sinking in the damp sand. My tortured insides responded to every jolt with a spasm.

I stopped by the tourist centre, leaning the bicycle against a wall.

Galina was by herself. My appearance did not startle her. She asked:

"Did you receive the telegram?"

I guess it would be hard to surprise anyone here with drunkenness.

I said:

"I need thirty roubles from the safe. I'll pay it back in two weeks. Just don't ask any questions."

"I know everything anyway. Your wife betrayed the motherland."

"Alas," I said.

"And now she is leaving for the West."

"It looks that way."

"And you are staying?"

"Yes, I am staying. As you know…"

"And you'll continue working?"

"Of course. If I don't get fired…"

"Is it true that only Jews live in Israel? Listen, are you ill? Would you like some water?"

"Water won't help. How about the money?"

"Only why from the safe? I have my own…"

I wanted to kiss Galina but held myself back. Her reaction could have been most unpredictable.

I got on the bicycle and went to the monastery.

The day was warm, but cloudy. The shadows of the trees were barely distinguishable from the grey asphalt. Tourists ambled along the side of the road. There were some that wore rainproof jackets.

I raced towards the sandy slope. I had a hard time holding on to the handlebars. Boulders tarnished by a coating of grey flew by...

The Ministry of the Interior's local branch was pointed out to me straight away.

"It's the building after the post office," the cleaner from The Seashore waved. "See that flag on the roof?"

I pedalled on.

The doors of the post office were wide open. Inside were two long-distance phone booths. One of them was occupied. A gesticulating blonde with big legs was shouting:

"Tata, do you hear? I wouldn't advise you to come... The weather here is B minus... But most importantly, there are absolutely no guys here... Hello, do you hear me? Lots of girls leave without feeling refreshed..."

I put on the brakes and pricked up my ears. Mentally I reached for the pen...

As dreadful as things looked, I was still alive. And, perhaps, the last thing to die in a man is his baseness. His ability to respond to peroxide blondes and the need to write...

On the steps of the ministry building, I ran into Guryanov. We nearly collided, so he couldn't avoid me.

At university, Guryanov was nicknamed Lenya the Snitch. His

main responsibility was keeping an eye on foreigners.

What's more, Guryanov was famous for his extraordinary ignorance. Once he was taking an oral exam with professor Byaly. Guryanov drew the question on the *Tales of Ivan Belkin*.*

Lenya attempted to broaden the theme. He opened on the subject of the Tsarist regime.

But the examiner asked:

"Have you read the *Tales of Ivan Belkin*?"

"Not really, I never had the occasion," replied Lenya. "Do you recommend it?"

"Yes." Byaly contained himself. "I strongly recommend that you read this book…"

Lenya came to see Byaly a month later and said:

"I've read it. Thank you. I liked a lot of it."

"And what did you like?" Byaly was curious.

Lenya tensed up, then remembered and said:

"The tale of *Ivan Onegin*…"

And here we ran into each other on the steps of the KGB.

At first he was a little taken aback. He wanted to walk away without saying hello. He lurched to the side, but it was difficult to miss each other on that porch. So he said:

"Well, hello, hello… Belyaev is waiting for you…"

He wanted to make it seem like everything was OK. As if we'd run into each other in a polyclinic and not the Gestapo.

I asked:

"Is he your boss?"

"Who?"

"Belyaev… Or a subordinate?"

"Don't be ironic," said Guryanov.

His voice had a firm, authoritative note.

"And remember, the KGB is the most progressive organization today. It's where the real power of the state is. And, by the way, the most humane... If you only knew what kind of people they are!"

"I'll know in a minute," I said.

"You're terribly infantile," said Guryanov. "It could end badly..."

This wasn't easy to listen to with a hangover!

I went past him, turned around and said:

"And you, Guryanov, are a piece of shit! You're a shit, an imbecile and a scoundrel! And you'll always be a scoundrel even if they make you a senior lieutenant... You know why you snitch? Because women don't like you..."

Guryanov capitulated as he stepped back. He tried to choose between indifference and superiority, but it ended in rancour.

I, however, felt great relief. And anyway, what could be better than an unexpected verbal release?

Guryanov hadn't prepared for insults. Which is why he suddenly started to speak in a normal and natural voice:

"It's easy to humiliate a comrade... But you don't know how it all happened..."

He switched to a sonorous whisper:

"I nearly got thrown in the locker as a kid. The authorities practically saved me. They got me into university. Now they're promising a residency permit. Because I'm from Kulunda... Have you been to Kulunda? It's a pleasure below average..."

"Ah," I said, "now it all makes sense... Kulunda changes everything..."

I'm forever listening to the outpourings of monsters. It must mean that I am predisposed to madmen...

"So long, Guryan, bear your heavy cross..."

I pushed the pretty pink button. A meagre woman of indeterminable age let me in. Without a word she ushered me into the adjoining room.

I saw a safe, a portrait of Dzerzhinsky* and brown drapes. Like the ones in the restaurant. So much so that I felt a little queasy.

I sat in an armchair and pulled out my cigarettes. For a minute or two, I sat in solitude. Then one of the curtains moved and a man of about thirty-six stepped out from behind it. With grave reproach, he said:

"Have I invited you to sit down?"

I stood up.

"Sit down."

I sat.

The man enunciated with even greater reproach:

"Have I invited you to smoke?"

I reached for the ashtray, but heard:

"Smoke..."

He than sat down and gave me a long, sad and almost tragic look. His smile expressed the world's imperfection and the heavy burden of responsibility for the sins of others. His face, though, remained ordinary, like an underwear button.

The portrait above his head seemed more inspired. (Only

halfway through our meeting did I suddenly realize that it was Anton Makarenko* and not Dzerzhinsky.)

Finally he said:

"Can you guess why I invited you here? You can't? Excellent. Ask me a question. To the point, soldier-like. 'Why did you invite me here, Belyaev?' And I'll answer you. Also to the point, soldier-like: 'I don't know.' I haven't the slightest idea. I feel that something's not right. I feel that the lad took a wrong turn. He's been led astray by the snaking road. Believe it or not, it's been keeping me up at nights. 'Tomka,' I say to my wife, 'a good lad has gone wrong. He needs help…' And my Tomka, she's a humanist. She yells: 'Vitalik, you must help. Have a character-building talk with him. It's a shame, the lad is one of ours. He's healthy on the inside. Don't resort to harsh disciplinary methods. The organization does not only punish. The organization enlightens…' And I yell: 'The international situation is complex. Capitalist encirclement is taking its toll. The lad has gone too far. Contributes to this… what's its name… *Continental*. Like that Radio Liberty… He's become a literary turncoat, a traitor as bad as Solzhenitsyn. And to top it all, he's been geezed up to the eyeballs with that windbag Valera… So his wife played a dirty trick, decided to go to Israel… So what, is he to be lit now till he turns blue?' In short, I'm confused…"

Belyaev continued to talk for another fifteen minutes. I swear I saw tears glisten in his eyes.

Then he threw a sideways glance at the door and produced glasses:

"Let's unwind a little. It's not bad for you… in moderation…"

His vodka was warm. We had cookies as a chaser.

The phone gave a shrill cry.

"Major Belyaev speaking... At four thirty? I'll be there... And tell the cops to mind their own business..."

He turned to me:

"Where were we? Do you think the organization hasn't noticed this bedlam? The organization notices everything, better than that academic Sakharov. But where's the realistic solution? In what? In a restoration of capitalism? Let's suppose I've read your vaunted samizdat. Just as much crap as in *Znamya* magazine.* Only everything's turned on its head. White is now black and black is white... Take, for instance, the problem of agriculture. Let's say we go ahead and abolish collective farms. We give the peasants their land and whatnot. But first, ask the peasants what they think. Do they even want this land? What the fuck do they need this damned land for? Ask that windbag Valera. Go to the villages around the Preserve. Old man Timokha is the only one who remembers how to harness a horse. And when to sow and what – they've all forgotten. They can't bake a simple loaf of bread... Besides, any peasant will swap this land for a half a pint of vodka in the blink of an eye. Let alone half a bottle..."

Belyaev took out the glasses again once and for all. He turned pink. His thoughts deviated towards dissidence with blistering speed.

Twice the phone rang. Belyaev pressed the button on the intercom:

"Valeria Yanovna! Hold all calls."

His speech became fast, temperamental and full of acrimony: "You know what'll bring on the end of Soviet rule? I'll tell you. The end will come from vodka. Today, I figure, about sixty per cent of the workforce are soused by the time evening comes. And the numbers are climbing. There'll come a day when everyone'll be juiced to the gills, without exception. From the run-of-the mill private to the Minister of Defence. From the lowly labourer to the Minister of Heavy Industry. Everyone, except two or three women, children and, possibly, Jews. Which is clearly insufficient for building communism... And the whole merry-go-round will grind to a halt. The factories, the plants, the machine and tractor stations. And before you know it, we'll be under a new Tatar-Mongol yoke. Only this time it'll come from the West. Headed by Comrade Kissinger..."

Belyaev looked at his watch:

"I know you're headed to Leningrad. My advice to you – don't make noise. To put it politely – zip your trap. The organization may teach and teach, but then it may suddenly be fool enough to punish. And your dossier packs more punch than Goethe's *Faust*. There's enough on you for forty years... And remember, a criminal case is not like a pair of seamed trousers. A criminal case is stitched together in five minutes. Blink, and you're on the front lines, building communism... So keep it down... And one more thing, about the boozing. Drink, but in moderation. Take a break now and then. And don't get involved with that nut job Markov. Valera is a local, they won't touch him. But your wife is in the West. Plus your opuses are in counter-revolutionary publications. And there are plenty of escapades to fill a dossier. If you don't behave, things might take a bad turn... In short, drink with caution. And now, one for the road..."

We had another drink.

"You may leave." The major switched to a more formal mode of address.

"Thank you," I said.

Those were the only words I spoke in half an hour.

Belyaev grinned:

"The conversation was conducted on a high ideological and political level."

At the door he added in a whisper:

"And one more thing, off the record, as they say. In your place, I'd bolt out of here while they're letting people go. Reunite with the wife – and best regards... I myself have no chance. No one will let me out with my yokel's mug... But you, that's my advice. Think about it. This is just between us, strictly confidential..."

I shook his hand, nodded to the surly woman and stepped out into the sunlit street.

I walked and thought, "Madness has taken over the world. Madness is becoming the norm." The norm brought on a sense of wonder...

I left the bicycle at the post office. I told them it was for Lyuda from Berezino. I climbed up the hill on foot. And finally, after waiting for an intercity bus, I left for Leningrad.

I fell asleep during the trip and woke up with a terrible headache...

Leningrad starts out gradually, with faded foliage, loud trams and gloomy brick buildings. In the morning light, the flickering neon letters are barely discernible. The faceless crowd cheers you up by its lack of interest.

Another minute and you are, once again, a city dweller. And only the sand in your shoes is a reminder of your summer in the country...

The headache stood in the way of my usual delight in the Leningrad clamour, the river breeze and clarity of the stone streets. The sidewalks alone, after the monotony of hills...

I got off the bus at Peace Square, hailed a cab, and fifteen minutes later I was home.

A laughing, unfamiliar woman in a sailor's jersey opened the door:

"The Shakhnoviches sent you? You've come for the coffee percolator?"

"No," I said.

"Is your last name Azarkh?"

"I'm Tanya's husband," I said...

Tanya came out, with a brown towel on her head. Our daughter appeared, pale, with frightened eyes:

"Oh, it's Papa..."

Our home was filled with mysterious characters. I only recognized Lazarev, a musicologist, and the black-marketeer, Beluga.

The apartment was noisy. A bald stranger was on the phone. He kept repeating:

"That has no practical importance..."

Everyone, in turns, was trying to speak to Tanya. A thin-bearded old man was almost screaming:

"Gentlemen, I trust we are all among friends here? Then please allow me to dismiss a conspiracy. I must get a message to Alexander Isayevich Solzhenitsyn..."

Then the old man articulated in a well-trained voice:

"I give permission to Solzhenitsyn to publish the unabridged version of my front-line poem 'Lucy'. All monies due to me I donate to the Solzhenitsyn Foundation. My real name cannot be used under any circumstances. My pen name is Andrei Kolymsky!"

Bottles huddled on the window sills. There were no visibly drunk people. Everyone here had something in common, even though they weren't all Jews. Someone was gathering unknown signatures, waving a green notepad.

There was a row of suitcases in the kitchen. These were identical new suitcases with metal locks. They filled me with hopelessness...

A guitar lay on the bed...

Words like "visa and registration", "HIAS",* "Berlin flight" and "customs declaration" accented the conversation.

I felt like a total outsider. And was even glad when a strange woman sent me downstairs to get tea.

Before that, I had a drink and felt a little better. There are dozens of books written about the harmful effects of alcohol. And not even a single brochure on the benefits. Which seems a mistake...

Several hours had gone by. Tanya was packing a camera she'd left out. Masha was giving away pebbles from the Black Sea to remember her by.

A few times they came up to me. We exchanged some meaningless words:

"Don't be sad, write... Everything will be fine..."

I knew that the nightmare would begin tomorrow. And then I had a thought – I'll get all the leftover booze...

Masha said:

"We've got dollars. Want to see?"

I said:

"Sure."

Then there was a discussion about some report on Israeli radio.

People came and went. Tanya wrote down addresses and instructions...

It wouldn't be complete without a scandal. The bald guy got drunk and shouted:

"So you're jumping off a sinking ship?"

Someone objected:

"So you're saying that the ship is sinking? And this is coming from a party member?"

"I'm not a party member," retorted the troublemaker. "I don't like that they're only letting out Jews!"

"Aren't you a Jew?"

"I'm a Jew," said the bald guy...

I waited for an appropriate moment and said:

"Tanya, when you're in the States, find Carl Proffer.* He wanted to publish my book."

"Should I tell him to do it?"

"Yes, and as quickly as possible. I've nothing to lose."

"I'll write you everything between the lines…"

Suddenly Lazarev announced that it was six o'clock. Time to go to the airport. We ordered several taxis and arrived there almost at the same time.

Tanya and Masha were whisked behind a barrier right away to fill out declarations. We strolled through the halls. Someone brought a bottle of vodka from home.

Beluga walked up to me and said:

"You're being a good sport, not losing your spirits."

I replied:

"That'd be all I need! I'll just get married again and make a bunch of kids."

Beluga shook his head with incredulity…

Tanya came to the barrier probably four times. She handed me things held back by customs. Including an amber necklace, my army photograph and a book by Gladilin,* signed by the author.

The fact that they removed my photograph made Misha Lazarev very angry. He said:

"What kind of antics are these? Where's the justice?"

Beluga interjected:

"If there was justice, what would be the point in leaving?"

I found a moment and said to Tanya:

"What do you think, will we see each other again?"

"Yes, I'm sure of it. Absolutely sure."

"Then maybe I'll believe that there is a God."

"We'll see each other again. There is a God…"

I wanted to believe her. I was ready to believe… But why should I have believed her now? After all, I didn't believe her when she said that Alberto Moravia* was a good writer...

Then we climbed onto some sort of balcony. We saw Tanya and Masha get on a bus.

Time stopped. These few seconds felt like a line between past and future.

The bus started.

Now I could go home, without saying goodbye...

For eleven days I drank in a locked apartment. Three times I went downstairs for more booze. If anyone phoned, I said: "I can't talk."

I lacked the resolve to unplug the phone. I'm forever waiting for something...

On the fourth day, the cops came. They knocked on the door early in the morning, even though there was a doorbell. Fortunately, the chain was on. A plastic visor gleamed through the crack in the door. I heard an assured and impatient hacking cough.

I did not fear the police. I simply couldn't talk to the authorities. My appearance alone was enough... I asked:

"What's going on? Show me a warrant... There is a law on search-and-seizures..."

The policeman said threateningly:

"A warrant's not a problem."

He left right away. And I returned to my bottles. Any one of which held a miracle.

Twenty minutes passed. Something made me look out the window. A police squad was marching across the yard. I think there were ten of them.

I heard their heavy footsteps on the stairway. Then they rang the doorbell, impatiently and insistently.

I ignored them.

What could they do? Break down an old Petersburg door? Everyone from Rubenstein Street would come running to the noise...

The policemen milled around outside the door for about an hour. One of them shouted through the keyhole:

"Provide an explanation according to the following articles of the Criminal Code: operating a brothel, parasitism, insubordination..."

There were so many articles, I decided not to think about it.

The policemen wouldn't leave. One of them proved to be a good psychologist. He knocked on the door and yelled:

"May I ask you for a glass of cold water?"

Apparently he was counting on my compassion. Or the magical power of the absurd.

I ignored them.

Finally, the cops slipped a piece of paper under the door and left. I saw how they crossed the yard. This time I counted them. Six visors beamed in the sun.

The piece of paper turned out to be a summons, which I examined for maybe three minutes. At the bottom it stated: "Attendance is mandatory." The investigator's name was missing. As was the name of the case file in connection with which I was being summoned. It didn't even say who I was: a witness, defendant or victim. And it didn't give a room number. Only a time and date.

I knew that a summons like this was invalid. Igor Yefimov put me wise to that. And I threw it in the garbage...

After that, the policemen showed up about four more times. And I always found out about it in advance. Smirnov, the alcoholic, warned me.

Gena Smirnov was a journalist down on his luck. He lived in the building across from mine. For days on end, he drank chartreuse by the window. And kept his eye out on the street, out of curiosity.

I lived deep inside the courtyard, on the fifth floor, without a lift. Our entrance was about a hundred yards from the gate.

If a police squad showed up in our yard, Smirnov would push aside the bottle and call me. He would articulate just the one single phrase:

"The bitches are coming!"

After which I would once more inspect the bolts and retreat to the kitchen. As far away from the front door as possible.

As the unit pulled away, I would peek out from behind the curtain. In the distant window opposite, Smirnov paced. He would salute me with his bottle...

On the eleventh day I began having hallucinations. These weren't demons, these were your garden-variety cats. White and grey. Several of them.

Then I got caught in a downpour of little worms. Red spots appeared on my stomach. The skin on the palms of my hands started to peel.

The booze ran out. The money ran out. I didn't have the strength to go anywhere or do anything.

What was left for me to do? Get into bed, pull the covers over my head and wait. Sooner or later all this had to end. My heart is strong. After all, it had seen me through a hundred benders.

The motor is good. Too bad the brakes are missing. I stop only when I hit a ditch.

I pulled the covers over my head and lay still. Mysterious slimy things swarmed around my feet. Faint little bells jingled in the gloom.

Numbers and letters marched in formation over my blanket. From time to time they formed short sentences. One time I read:

"Only death is final!"

Not such a silly thought, if you think about it.

At this moment, the phone rang. I knew who it was right away. I knew it was Tanya. I just knew and that's all.

I lifted the receiver. Out of the chaos came Tanya's calm voice:

"Hi! We're in Austria. Everything's fine... Were you drinking?"

I got angry:

"Who do you take me for?"

"We were met at the airport. There are a lot of friends here. Everyone sends their regards."

I was standing barefoot by the phone without saying anything. A radiogram roared outside the window. There was a reflection of an old coat in the mirror.

I only asked:

"Will we see each other again?"

"Yes... If you love us..."

I didn't even ask where. It didn't matter. In heaven, perhaps. Because heaven is just that, a meeting place and nothing more.

A general holding cell where you can meet your loved ones...

Suddenly I saw the world as a whole. Everything was happening at the same time. Everything was unfolding before my eyes...

My wife said:

"Yes, if you love us..."

"What does love have to do with it?" I asked.

And added:

"Love is for the young. It is for soldiers and athletes... Things are much more complicated here. It's beyond love. It's fate..."

Then something clicked and there was silence.

Now I would have to go to sleep in an empty and stuffy room...

— June 1983
New York

Afterword

"POLITICAL WORK OUGHT TO BE CONCRETE": this is one of the rousing Soviet mottos recalled in Sergei Dovlatov's novel, *The Zone*. Ironically, it is also what is said about good writing, and can one think of a more concrete contemporary writer than Dovlatov? Sentences compacted to aphoristic ingots: "One is born either poor or rich. Money has almost nothing to do with it." Paradox, sharp wit, and swift one-liners: "Boris sober and Boris drunk are such different people, they've never even met." Or: "What could I say to him? What do you say to a guard who uses after-shave only internally?" Fierce, precise snapshots, illuminated by absurdist flashes: "Cars streamed past us like submarines holding each other's tails." Dialogue almost Waugh-like in its tart comedy:

"You've just forgotten. The rudeness, the lies."
"If people are rude in Moscow, at least it's in Russian."
"That's the horrible part."

And people, things, clothes, memories, stories – all seized and made instantly vivid:

Indistinct memories came to him.
…A square in winter, tall rectangular buildings. A few

school-boys surround Vova Mashbits, the class telltale. Vova's expression is frightened, he wears a foolish hat, woollen drawers... Koka Dementiyev tears a grey sack out of his hand. Shakes a pair of galoshes out onto the snow. After which, faint with laughter, he urinates into the sack. The schoolboys grab Vova, hold him by the shoulders, shove his head into the darkened sack. The boy stops trying to break loose. It's not actually painful...

Reading Dovlatov is a joyous, thrilling, usually hilarious experience, in large part because he has such a talent for making stories so concrete: he collects vignettes, loud portraits, bitter jokes, comic tales, absurd episodes, black anecdotes, and then delights in bringing them out of the ether of hearsay or memory and giving them new life in print. He captures, and he frees: his work bursts with this captured, freed life. There is the prisoner Makeyev, in *The Zone*, who climbs onto the roof of the prison camp to watch the woman he has fallen in love with, a schoolteacher named Isolda Shchukina. [119] He is unable to make out her features or even her age. He knows only that she wears two dresses, a green one and a brown one: "Early in the morning, Makeyev would crawl onto the roof of the barracks. After some time, there would be a thunderous announcement: 'Brown!' This meant that Isolda had gone out to visit the toilet facilities." [119] There is the story, from *The Suitcase*, of the Lenin statue that went wrong. People gather for the unveiling of the new monument; a band plays, speeches are given. And as a drum rolls, the cloth is lifted – to reveal Lenin in familiar pose, his right arm pointing "the way to the future" and his left in the pocket of his open coat. The music stops, and suddenly someone laughs. "A minute later, the whole crowd was laughing... What had happened? The poor sculptor had given Lenin two caps, one on the leader's head, the other one clutched in his fist." [24] In the same book, Dovlatov remembers being asked to play Old Grandfather Frost in a New Year's show for a school. He is promised three days off and fifteen rubles. On stage, he appears in a beard, a white hat, and bearing a basket of gifts. "Hello, dear children! Do you recognize me?" And the yelled reply comes from the front rows: "Lenin! Lenin!" [115]

There are the sparkling sketches, in A Foreign Woman, of Russian émigrés in New York – like Fima Druker, a famous bibliophile when he lived in Leningrad, now running a publishing company called Russian Book, which struggles to survive in America, and which is eventually renamed Invisible Book (apparently now specializing in erotica); or Zaretsky, a journalist notorious in the Soviet Union for his "voluminous" work published in samizdat, Sex Under Totalitarianism, "which claimed that ninety per cent of Soviet women were frigid." [8] At one point in the novel, Zaretsky attempts to do some sex research on the novel's heroine, an émigré named Marusya Tatarovich: one of his questions involves asking her if she lost her virginity "before or after the Hungarian events." [48]

Sergei Dovlatov was born in 1941, in Ufa, in the Republic of Bashkiria; his family had been evacuated there from Leningrad during the Second World War. His mother was Armenian, his father Jewish and a distinguished theater director. His intensely autobiographical work – warmly and casually mixing fiction and fact; often jocosely combining fiction with what postmodernism calls metafiction (that is, commentary on fiction-making) – offers the reader a vital picture of the usual bald biographical summary. In his writing, including this book, we learn about the many phases of his short life (he died in 1990, in New York City): about his parents and their work in the theater (the wonderful story, "Fernand Léger's Jacket"); about the time he spent, in the early 1960s, as a prison guard in the Soviet camp system (*The Zone*); about his work as a journalist, in Leningrad and Estonia (*The Suitcase* and *The Compromise*); the summer he spent as an official guide at the Pushkin Preserve, south of Pskov (*Pushkin Hills*).

Dovlatov was not published in Russia during his lifetime. During the 1970s, he circulated his writing in samizdat and began to be published in European journals, an activity which brought about his expulsion from the Union of Soviet Journalists in 1976. He left the Soviet Union in 1978 and arrived in New York in 1979 to join his wife and daughter, part of the so-called "third wave" of Russian immigration (an anxious transit anticipated in *Pushkin Hills* and more fully described in *A Foreign Woman* and the memoir, *Ours*, which traces the stories of four generations of his family). In New York, Dovlatov quickly became one of the most prominent and popular members of the Russian émigré community. He co-edited *The New American*, a liberal émigré newspaper, and worked for Radio Liberty. But mainly he wrote: twelve books in the last twelve years of his life. *The Compromise* appeared in 1981, *The Zone* a year

later, *Ours* in 1983, *A Foreign Woman* in 1986, the same year
that *The Suitcase* was published. These books were written in
Russian and published by small presses, such as the Hermitage
Press in Tenafly, New Jersey, or Russica, in New York. It was
only in the mid-1980s, when Dovlatov was beginning to reach
a wider audience (partly due to the publication of several of his
stories in *The New Yorker*), that English-language publishers
took an interest: *The Zone* was published in English translation in 1985 (Knopf) and *The Suitcase* in 1990 (Weidenfeld).

One of those books, *Pushkin Hills,* appeared in 1983 under
the title *Zapovednik* ("The Preserve"). It has waited thirty years
for its publication in English in this brilliant translation by the
writer's daughter, Katherine Dovlatov. Like all of Dovlatov's
work, it has charm, bite, vitality, and a peculiar sweetness. The
book is narrated by an authorial alter ego, Boris Alikhanov, a
youngish, unpublished writer with a drinking problem, who is
spending the summer as a guide at Pushkin's house and estate
near Pskov. In *The Zone*, his book about his experiences as a
prison guard, Dovlatov wrote that he deliberately refrained from
writing about "the wildest, bloodiest, most monstrous episodes
of camp life" – partly for moral and aesthetic reasons and partly
because, he added mordantly, he did not want to be known as
a Shalamov or Solzhenitsyn, writers best-known for their chill-
ing descriptions of Gulag life. "I absolutely do not want to be
known as the modern-day Virgil who leads Dante through hell
(however much I may love Shalamov). It's enough that I worked
as a guide on the Pushkin estate." [163] In that book, Dovlatov
argued that a Soviet camp was Soviet society in a microcosm,

and one of the teasing pleasures of *Pushkin Hills* is the jokey way he treats the Pushkin estate as both a benign prison camp and another microcosmic analogue of Soviet reality – complete with ambitious apparatchiks, loyal ideologues, ornery peasants, loathsome snitches, and dissident intellectuals (i.e. Dovlatov himself, in the guise of Boris Alikhanov). Of course, because this is the benign, literary version, the apparatchiks and ideologues are all Pushkin devotees who cannot countenance anything but utter devotion to the literary idol. Marianna Petrovna, whose job at the estate is the daunting-sounding "methodologist," gives Boris the once-over:

"Do you love Pushkin?"
I felt a muffled irritation.
"I do."
At this rate, I thought, it won't be long before I don't.
"And may I ask you why?"...
"What do you mean?" I asked.
"Why do you love Pushkin?"
"Let's stop this idiotic test," I burst out. [24]

There are the familiar Dovlatov portraits, full of tender comedy: Mitrofanov, for instance, a guide famous for his photographic memory, who has read ten thousand books, but who has become incurably lazy. He suffers, says Dovlatov, from aboulia, or "total atrophy of the will": "He was a phenomenon that belonged to the vegetable kingdom, a bright, fanciful flower. A chrysanthemum cannot hoe its own soil and water itself." [48] Strangely, life at the Pushkin preserve suits Mitrofanov, and he delivers fanatically detailed and scholarly lectures to largely ungrateful tourists. Or Guryanov, famous for his extraordinary ignorance, who once confused Pushkin's *Tales of Ivan Belkin* with what he absurdly called "The tale of *Ivan Onegin*"...[124] Or Mikhail Ivanych Sorokin, the rustic alcoholic in whose revoltingly neglected hovel Boris rents a room for the season, and who wants to be paid not in cash but in booze and cigarettes.

Like everything Dovlatov wrote, *Pushkin Hills* is funny on every page, sparkling with jokes, repartee, and this writer's special savage levity. But Dovlatov is also expert at what Gogol called "laughter through tears." In *Pushkin Hills*, the almost Wodehouse-like escapades in the countryside are constantly menaced by the obligations and difficulties Boris has fled – how to be a writer in the Soviet Union, how to live amicably with his wife and daughter. "Officially, I was a full-fledged creative personality. In reality, I was on the edge of a mental breakdown." [79] These anxieties present themselves in concentrated form when Boris's wife, Tanya, begins to force the question of emigration. On a surprise visit to the Pushkin estate, she tells Boris that she has made the decision: she will file emigration papers next week. Boris is fearful, irrational, resistant. He refuses to leave the Soviet Union. He loves his country – "My language, my people, my crazy country...Imagine this, I even love the policemen." [86] Emigration seems like death to him; he tells Tanya that in a foreign tongue "we lose eighty percent of our personality." [87] America seems merely fictional, chimerical: "A half-forgotten film starring Akbar the tiger and Charlie Chaplin..." [88]

Boris seems to anticipate the émigré life that Dovlatov would write about three years later in *A Foreign Woman*, a book which, like *Pushkin Hills*, is full of jollity and tremulous sadness. In that later book several of the characters struggle to adapt to life in New York – people like Karavayev, for instance, known in the Soviet Union as a brave human rights activist (imprisoned three times and a serial hunger striker). America, writes Dovlatov, had "disappointed" Karavayev: "He missed the Soviet regime, Marxism, and the punitive organs. Karavayev had nothing to protest against." [10] The heroine of *A Foreign Woman*, Marusya Tatarovich, decides that she has made a mistake in leaving Russia and applies to return. Dovlatov (who appears as himself in this book) asks her about the prospect of losing her newfound freedom. "To hell with freedom! I want peace!" Raised in relative privilege in the Soviet Union, she has feeble economic prospects in New York: "Wash dishes in a lousy restaurant? Study computers? Sell chestnuts on 108ᵗʰ Street? I'd rather go back." [82] At the Soviet embassy, she is told that it is all very well to confess in private to having made a mistake, but if she wants to return she must now "earn forgiveness." (A political, nicely comic version of Dostoevsky's idea that the criminal must religiously "accept his suffering.") Marusya is told she will have to write a newspaper article laying out her errors as public atonement. But she can't write journalism, she says. Who will pen the piece? "I'll get Dovlatov to write it." Needless to say, the article remains unwritten; for better or worse, Marusya stays in America.

In its sly, sidelong, defiantly non-aligned way, Dovlatov's work is always probing questions of freedom. Boris, in *Pushkin Hills*, perhaps belongs on a spectrum with Karavayev and Marusya Tatarovich in *A Foreign Woman* and in *The Zone*, Chichevanov, a prisoner who escapes from camp just hours before his legitimate release – after twenty years inside, he is so afraid of freedom that he wants only to be recaptured. "Outside the prison gates," says one of the officers, Chichevanov "would have had nothing to do. He was wildly afraid of freedom, he was gasping for breath like a fish." And Dovlatov adds: "There's something similar in what we Russian émigrés experience." [88]

It's not simply that freedom might be frightening, novel, unreal; it's that it might turn out to be not as free as advertised – or not free in exactly the way promised. And if you refuse to risk the potential "disappointment" of freedom by exercising it, you will, at least, avoid *that* disappointment. It's why Boris fearfully defends, even to the point of absurdity, his non-existent status as Russian writer: when Tanya reminds him that he hasn't been (and, seemingly, can't be) published in the Soviet Union, he replies, "But my readers are here. While over there...Who needs my stories in Chicago?" [87] Better, perhaps, to have always-unrealized potential than lapsed actuality. Shadowing Boris, and indeed all of Dovlatov's émigrés, is the double sense of freedom, both positive and negative, that V.S. Naipaul beautifully evokes at the end of his story "One out of Many," from *In a Free State*. The story is about Santosh, a poor servant from Bombay who accompanies his master, a diplomat, to Washington, D.C. Santosh is utterly lost in America, but he eventually marries an African-American woman and thus gains the right to stay. His new employer, who owns an Indian restaurant, reassures him that in the States no one cares, as they would in India, that Santosh is married to a black woman: "Nobody looks at you when you walk down the street. Nobody cares what you do." And Santosh comments: "He was right. I was a free man; I could do anything I wanted...It didn't matter what I did, because I was alone." It is an enormous privilege to live in a country where "nobody cares what you do"; but when nobody cares what you do, then perhaps it doesn't matter what you do. Perhaps apprehending something like this, Boris falters and freezes; it is easier to make no decision at all. He lets his wife and daughter go ahead of him.

Freedom is both actual and ideal, both concrete and metaphysical. There are enacted realities, like the rule of law, free speech, economic possibility and limitation, material circumstance – it should go without saying that these actualities are of enormous consequence in immigrants' lives. But the émigré has also a strange, pure, almost metaphysical liberty: this, as Nabokov knew, is the portable, remembered world he or she brings with him from the old country. Nabokov's émigré professor, Timofey Pnin, knows this portable, internal, untouchable, *undisappointable* world to be the cosmos you carry inside you – the stories, the people, the memories, the anecdotes and jokes, even the very dates of one's national history; in short, the émigré's entire cultural formation: "a brilliant cosmos that seemed all the fresher for having been abolished by one blow of history," as Pnin thinks of it. It is why Dovlatov is able to look at the single suitcase he brought with him from the Soviet

Union and disdain the things inside it (the hat, the jacket, the shirt, the gloves). The things are not important. What are important are the stories these things drag with them, the very stories Dovlatov made into his book, *The Suitcase*, the stories that enliven every page of his writing. In this sense, things are not concrete; the impalpable stories are, made so by the great writer when set down brilliantly, vividly in print for generations of future readers. I don't know if Boris quite understands this, at the end of *Pushkin Hills*; but we are very fortunate that Sergei Dovlatov did.

—James Wood

Notes

p. 7, *Gordin, Shchegolev, Tsyavlovskaya... Kern's memoirs*: Arkady Gordin (1913–97) was a Pushkin expert who wrote a number of books on Pushkin in Mikhailovskoye, where the Pushkin Preserve is now located. Pavel Shchegolev (1877–1931) and Tatyana Tsyavlovskaya (1897–1978) were also noted Pushkin specialists. Anna Kern (1800–79) was briefly Pushkin's lover. The two met in nearby Trigorskoye in 1825.

p. 8, *Alexei Vulf's Diaries*: Alexei Nikolayevich Vulf (1805–81) was a bon vivant and close friend of Pushkin.

p. 8, *Ryleyev's mother*: Kondraty Ryleyev (1795–1826) was a leader in the Decembrist Revolt of 1825, which sought to overthrow the Tsar, and a publisher of Pushkin's work.

p. 13, *Hannibal... Zakomelsky*: Ibrahim Hannibal (1696–1781) was Pushkin's great-grandfather, an African (probably from modern-day Eritrea) who was kidnapped as a child and given as a gift to the Russian tsar, later becoming a high-ranking favourite of Peter the Great. Pushkin wrote an unfinished novel, *The Negro of Peter the Great*, on the subject of Hannibal. There is a famous painting that was traditionally thought to depict Hannibal, though some scholars have argued that the medal depicted in the painting was an order not created until after Hannibal's death. Baron Ivan Mellor–Zakomelsky (1725–90), the putative subject of the painting, was a high-ranking general who served in the Second Russo-Turkish War.

p. 15, *The Bronze Horseman*: Pushkin's 1833 narrative poem which takes its title from a statue of Peter the Great in St Petersburg.

p. 17, *Likhonosov*: Viktor Likhonosov (1936–) was closely associated with the "Village Prose" literary movement of the Sixties that focused on rural life in the Soviet Union and often presented a nostalgic or idealized view of Russia.

p. 18, *Mandelstam*: Osip Mandelstam (1891–1938), Russian poet and essayist.

p. 19, *the writer Volin's work*: Probably Vladimir Volin (1924–98), writer and journalist who worked for a variety of Soviet magazines and journals.

p. 20, *Gleb Romanov... in Bucharest*: Gleb Romanov (1920–67) was a popular actor and performer. Ruzhena Sikora (1918–2006) was a well-known Soviet singer of Czech origin. "This song for two *soldi*" is a line from the song 'Una canzone da due soldi' by the Italian singer Achille Togliani (1924–95). 'I Daydreamt of You in Bucharest' was a Russian song from the Fifties performed by Sidi Tal (1912–83), a Jewish singer popular in the Soviet Union.

p. 23, *The sacred path will not be overgrown*: A deliberate distortion of Pushkin's famous poem 'Exegi monumentum': "the people's path will not be overgrown". Dovlatov famously attempted never to have two words in one sentence begin with the same letter – Pushkin's text "*ne zarastyot narodnaya tropa*" has two Ns.

p. 27, *Agdam*: An Azeri fortified white wine.

p. 30, *the Order of the Red Star*: A decoration given for

exceptional military bravery, or for long service in the armed forces.

p. 31, *Gagarin*: Yuri Gagarin (1934–68), Soviet cosmonaut and the first human to travel into outer space.

p. 34, *The Decembrist uprising*: The failed attempt to overthrow the Tsar in 1825, directly supported by many of Pushkin's close friends.

p. 34, *Benois*: Alexandre Benois (1870–1960) was a Russian artist who worked extensively with the Ballets Russes and Sergei Diaghilev.

p. 36, *Yesenin... Pasternak*: Sergei Yesenin (1895–1925), a Russian lyrical poet who committed suicide at the age of thirty. His works were widely celebrated, but many were banned by the authorities. The poet and novelist Boris Pasternak (1890–1960) suffered enormously at the hands of the authorities, especially after being awarded the Nobel Prize for Literature in 1958 for the novel *Doctor Zhivago*, which was banned in the Soviet Union.

p. 36, *Solzhenitsyn's*: Alexander Solzhenitsyn (1914–2008), dissident writer and activist.

p. 38, *the famous drawing by Bruni*: In 1837, Fyodor Bruni (1799–1875) sketched Pushkin on his deathbed.

p. 38, *the secret removal and funeral... Alexander Turgenev*: Alexander Turgenev (1784–1846), a close friend of Pushkin's, transported the poet's body to the family vault in Svyatogorsky Monastery, near Mikhailovskoye.

p. 39, *Kramskoy's Portrait of a Woman on the wall*: Ivan Kramskoy (1837–87), Russian painter and critic.

p. 40, *Intercession*: The Intercession of the Theotokos, a holy day in the Russian Orthodox Church, celebrated on 1st October.

p. 42, *1917... Makhno*: Nestor (or Bat'ko, a diminutive of the word "father") Makhno (1888–1934) was a Ukrainian anarchist who fought against both the Whites and Reds in the Russian Civil War. Although Makhno escaped the Cheka (the Soviet secret police) after the Bolsheviks consolidated their power, many of his followers were shot.

p. 42, *What was the duel between Pushkin and Lermontov about?*: Pushkin and Lermontov, the best-known poets of nineteenth-century Russia, both died famously in duels, but not with one another. It is believed they never even met.

p. 42, *Pikul, Rozhdestvensky, Meylakh... Novikov*: Valentin Savvich Pikul (1928–90) was a writer of popular historical novels. Robert Ivanovich Rozhdestvensky (1932–94) was a lyrical poet. Boris Solomonovich Meylakh (1909–87) was a literary critic who specialized in Pushkin. Ivan Alexeyevich Novikov (1877–1959) was a prolific author who wrote several works on Pushkin.

p. 43, *Benckendorff*: Alexander von Benckendorff (c.1782–1844) was a Russian commander and later directly monitored and censored Pushkin's correspondence and literary work.

p. 44, *Arina Rodionovna... Seryakov*: Arina Rodionovna Yakovleva (1758–1828) was Pushkin's nanny. Yakov Seryakov (1818–69) was a sculptor.

p. 44, *a Finnish knife flashed ominously*: Another reference from Yesenin's 'Letter to Mother' (1924).

p. 45, *Mnemosyne... Delvig*: Mnemosyne was a short-lived literary journal founded by Wilhelm Karlovich Küchelbecker (1797–1846) and Vladimir Fyodorovich Odoevsky (1803–69). Anton Antonovich Delvig (1798–1831), poet and close friend of Pushkin.

p. 45, *Sergei Lvovich... Sergei Alexandrovich*: The narrator has confused the patronymics of Pushkin's father and Yesenin.

p. 46, *Suprematism*: A Russian art movement of the mid-1910s which focused on geometric patterns.

p. 47, *Talleyrand... Lomonosov's wife*: Charles Maurice de Talleyrand-Périgord (1754–1838), famed diplomat and statesman. Mikhail Lomonosov (1711–65), pioneering Russian grammarian, poet, scientist and founder of Moscow State University.

p. 52, *d'Anthès*: Georges-Charles d'Anthès (1812–95) killed Pushkin in a duel in 1837, in a dispute over Pushkin's wife.

p. 55, *Kiprensky... in a looking glass*: Orest Kiprensky (1782–1836) was a leading figure in Russian portraiture, and painted one of the most famous portraits of Pushkin. The verse quoted is from an 1827 poem Pushkin dedicated to Kiprensky on seeing the portrait.

p. 55, *Godunov... Gypsies... if you love my shadow*: All from Pushkin's oeuvre. *Boris Godunov*, a drama, was published in 1831. *The Gypsies* was a long narrative poem published in 1827. The quotation comes from Pushkin's 1825 elegy to the French poet André Chénier.

p. 56, *Gukovsky and Shchegolev*: Grigory Alexandrovich Gukovsky (1902–50) was a Formalist literary historian. For

Shchegolev see first note to p. 7.

p. 58, *Likhonosov*: See note to p. 17.

p. 59, *the Remizov school of writing*: Alexei Remizov (1877–1957), a Russian symbolist writer with an unusual style and a fixation on the whimsical and grotesque.

p. 71, *Nefertiti*: Nefertiti (*c.*1370–*c.*1330 BC), wife of the Egyptian pharaoh Akhenaten.

p. 75, *Thou, nature, art my goddess*: Spoken by Edmund in *King Lear*, Act 1, Sc. 2.

p. 78, *Comrade Grishin*: Presumably Viktor Grishin (1914–92), First Secretary of the Moscow Central Committee from 1967 to 1985.

p. 79, *an appealing ethnic minority... Granin and Rytkheu*: Presumably Dovlatov is referring here to his Armenian background. Yuri Rytkheu (1930–2008) was a Russian and Chukchi writer. Daniil Granin (1919–) is a Russian writer and public figure.

p. 82, *Bulgarin*: Faddey Bulgarin (1789–1859), a reactionary journalist and writer whom Pushkin disliked.

p. 86, *Heifetz*: The dissident writer Mikhail Heifetz (1934–).

p. 86, *Grani. Or Continent*: Émigré dissident journals dealing with art and politics.

p. 86, *Bukovsky... Kuznetsov*: Vladimir Bukovsky (1942–) and Anatoly Kuznetsov (1929–79), dissident writers.

p. 88, *Santa María*: One of the ships that Christopher Columbus used on his voyage to the New World in 1492.

p. 92, *Anatoly Korolyov*: Anatoly Korolyov (1942–91), a popular singer in the Soviet Union.

p. 93, *do widzenia*: "Goodbye" (Polish).

p. 105, *Kobzon... Tsvetaeva*: Iosif Kobzon (1937–), Russian crooner; Marina Tsvetaeva (1892–1941), one of the best-known lyrical poets of twentieth-century Russia.

p. 108, *Baba Yaga*: A famous character in Russian fairy tales, an evil witch who lives in a hut on chicken legs.

p. 110, *Viscount de Bragelonne*: *The Viscount of Bragelonne* (1847–50) is a novel by Alexandre Dumas *père* (1802–70).

p. 111, *I accede, like Shepilov*: In the plot to oust Khrushchev in 1957, Dmitri Shepilov (1905–95), a secretary of the Central Committee, sided with the anti-Khrushchev faction led by Molotov, Malenkov, Kaganovich, Pervukhin and Saburov, who were swiftly defeated and lost all political influence and posts.

p. 112, *Kursk Magnetic Anomaly*: A region in central Russia rich in iron ore.

p. 113, *Karatsupa*: Nikita Karatsupa (1910–94) was a renowned border guard in the Soviet Union, who was said to have captured countless spies and smugglers, worked extreme hours and was decorated with the Order of Lenin, the highest decoration in the USSR.

p. 116, *Article 92, without an instrument*: Presumably a reference to the non-violent theft of state property.

p. 116, *Finita la commedia*: "The comedy is over" (Italian).

p. 117, *Ogonyok magazine*: A popular illustrated political and social magazine.

p. 117, *Julius Fučík*: Julius Fučík (1872–1916) was a Czech composer of predominantly military and patriotic marches.

p. 118, *the academic Sakharov*: Andrei Sakharov (1921–89), nuclear physicist who contributed significantly to the development of the Soviet hydrogen bomb, who later became an outspoken dissident and human-rights activist.

p. 119, *Baratynsky*: Yevgeny Baratynsky (1800–44) was a Russian poet and contemporary of Pushkin.

p. 124, *the Tales of Ivan Belkin*: A collection of five short stories by Pushkin, published in 1831.

p. 126, *Dzerzhinsky*: Felix Dzerzhinsky (1877–1926), or "Iron Felix", established the notorious Soviet secret police, the Cheka, shortly after the October Revolution of 1917.

p. 127, *Anton Makarenko*: Makarenko (1888–1939) was a Soviet educator and the founder of orphanages for children displaced by the Russian Civil War.

p. 128, *samizdat… Znamya magazine*: The term samizdat, derived from the Russian for "self-publishing", refers to the clandestine publication of literature not permitted by the authorities. *Znamya* is a literary periodical.

p. 132, *HIAS*: The Hebrew Immigrant Aid Society, a charity established in 1881 to assist Jews who were forced to emigrate from Russia.

p. 133, *Carl Proffer*: Professor of Russian at the University of Michigan, Carl Proffer (1938–84) co-founded the publishing house Ardis, which specialized in Russian literature not tolerated by the Soviet authorities, both in translation and in the original.

p. 134, *Gladilin*: Anatoly Gladilin (1935–), Russian writer who defected in the 1970s from Russia to live in Paris.

p. 135, *Alberto Moravia*: Alberto Moravia (1907–90), Italian writer and journalist.

Acknowledgements

The translator wishes to thank the following:

Amy Flanagan, for finding the time in her Blackberry-dominated life to correct my grammar. Alex Billington, for adding polish to the text. Beth Knobel and Marti Whelan, for the encouragement. Facebook friends, for the support and humour. Kirill Belyaninov, for his encyclopedic knowledge of Soviet prison jargon. Andrey Aryev for his intellectual generosity. My father, for leaving behind an amazing gift that allows us to continue a dialogue.

And my mother, who was right.